Countdown to Christmas

Dianna Houx

Copyright © 2022 by Dianna Houx

No part of this book may be used or reproduced by any means, graphic, electronic, or mechanical, including photocopying, recording, taping, or by any information storage retrieval system without the written permission of the publisher except in the case of brief quotations embodied in critical articles and reviews.

This is a work of fiction. Names, characters, businesses, places, events, locales, and incidents are either the products of the author's imagination or used in a fictitious manner. Any resemblance to actual persons, living or dead, or actual events is purely coincidental.

Contents

1. -Days till Christmas-   1
   Twenty
2. -Days till Christmas-   9
   Nineteen
3. -Days till Christmas-   19
   Eighteen
4. -Days till Christmas-   29
   Seventeen
5. -Days till Christmas-   39
   Sixteen
6. -Days till Christmas-   51
   Fifteen
7. -Days till Christmas-   57
   Fourteen

8.	-Days till Christmas- Thirteen	67
9.	-Days till Christmas- Twelve	77
10.	-Days till Christmas- Eleven	85
11.	-Days till Christmas- Ten	95
12.	-Days till Christmas- Nine	105
13.	-Days till Christmas- Eight	113
14.	-Days till Christmas- Seven	123
15.	-Days till Christmas- Six	133
16.	-Days till Christmas- Five	143
17.	-Days till Christmas- Four	153
18.	-Days till Christmas- Three	163

19.	-Days till Christmas- Two	173
20.	-Days till Christmas- One	183
21.	-Merry Christmas-	193
About the Author		201
Afterword		202

-Days till Christmas-

Twenty

"Can you believe it? Only twenty more days until Christmas!" Grace announced in a sing-song voice as she walked into Granny Josephine's room. "I can hardly wait!"

She set the tray she had been carrying on the bed next to her granny, careful not to spill the contents. "I brought you your favorite: chicken soup, grilled cheese, and a nice hot cup of chamomile tea," she said cheerfully.

"Thank you, dear girl," Granny said, reaching for the cup of tea with shaky hands. "You spoil me."

Grace watched as Granny struggled to eat, desperately wishing there was something she could do to help. They had been to numerous doctors over the last few months, but none had answers. Granny's health was obviously deteriorating, but no one could figure out why. Yes, she was up there in age, but eighty-five was not an automatic death sentence.

The last doctor they had seen had pulled Grace aside and explained that unless a miracle occurred, this Christmas was likely to be Granny's last. Devastated at losing her granny, the only family she had left, Grace had vowed to make this Christmas the best one they ever had. The only problem was she needed to figure out how to do that.

When Granny finished her food, Grace removed the tray and sat beside her on the bed. Taking her cold hands in hers, she asked. "Granny, will you tell me a story from your childhood?"

Granny smiled up at her. "Of course, my dear. I never could say no to you," she said, squeezing Grace's hands.

"My grandparents built this house in eighteen ninety-five when Winterwood was a booming railroad town. I know it's hard to imagine that a town of only two thousand was once a booming metropolis, but it was."

Grace watched as Granny's face took on a dreamy expression, as if she was picturing the past in her mind as she spoke.

"Grandpa Arthur built this house for my grandma, Ellen, and their six children. At that time, it was truly something special. This old place could have rivaled the Vanderbilt's or Rockefeller's mansions up north!" she chuckled.

"By the time I came along, forty years later, this old house had seen its share of love and loss. The six children had their own children, filling this place to the brim at holidays. We didn't mind, though; we loved it, in fact. Us kids had so much fun running around together, causing mischief."

Grace smiled at the twinkle in Granny's eyes. "It's hard to imagine you causing trouble," Grace laughed.

"Oh, you know how kids can be. There were over twenty cousins, all driving our mama's crazy. They used to come up with ideas to keep us busy and out of their hair."

"What kind of ideas?"

"Well, they used to let us decorate the Christmas cookies. That would keep us busy for at least ten minutes. Then the food fight would start, and we all ended up with more icing on us than on the cookies! Our mamas did not find it funny one bit, but we would just laugh and laugh. You would think they would have learned their lesson after the first time, but it became a tradition we did every year."

"And every year, it ended in a food fight?"

"Of course! We kids were not one to break with tradition! Although, I suspect our mamas weren't quite as upset with us as they claimed to be," she said with a wink.

Grace could see Granny getting a little color in her usually pale cheeks. Her voice got stronger as she reminisced. For the first time in months, she started to feel a little bit of hope. Which gave her an idea. "What other kinds of things did you do?"

"Oh, let's see. Each year, we were allowed to choose one ornament for the Christmas tree and decorate it however we liked. When it snowed, they sent us outside to go sledding, which usually ended in a snowball fight! And, of course, there was the annual snowman competition. The winner got to place the angel on the top of the Christmas tree," she said wistfully.

"That all sounds wonderful, Granny!" Grace said, clapping her hands together gleefully.

Granny chuckled. "That's only half of it. Winterwood was so magical back then. Each year, the town would transform into a real Christmas wonderland. There was an ice skating rink, a tree-lighting ceremony, and a parade. All the business owners down Main Street would dress their shops like something out of Santa's village. And, of course, Santa himself would show up to talk to all of us boys and girls. I do so miss those days," she sighed.

Grace tried to picture all of that in her mind. She had come to live with Granny twenty years ago, her parents having died in a car accident when she was five. In all those years, she had never seen her town come close to the image Granny described. It was time for things to change.

"Granny, I need to go out for a little bit tonight. I'll have Gladys from next door come over and watch Wheel of Fortune with you, okay?"

"You don't have to do that. I'll be fine by myself. It's good to see you getting out of here for a while. You spend way too much time caring for this old bag of bones!"

"Granny! Don't say things like that!" Grace exclaimed. "I know you can take care of yourself, but I also know that you like to have friendly little competitions with Gladys to see who can solve the puzzles first! You'll have much more fun if she's here while I'm gone."

Granny appeared to think about it. "I suppose...yes, go ahead and ask Gladys to come over. I'm in the mood for a little competition!"

Grace smiled, thrilled at the flash of spark she could see in Granny's attitude. If she kept this up, she might just get that Christmas miracle.

***

Grace walked into the town hall/community center/fire department just in time for the monthly town hall meeting. While it was true there were a little over two thousand residents in Winterwood, only a handful showed up for these meetings. Because of that, the mayor, the town council, and the few residents who came usually just sat in a circle.

Taking a seat in one of the few available chairs, Grace sighed and looked around. This was a little more intimidating than she thought it would be.

Mayor Allen looked up and smiled when he noticed her. "Grace, it's so good to see one of our younger residents taking an interest in town politics! How's Granny Parker doing?"

"That's actually why I'm here," she replied, taking a deep breath.

"Oh?" The mayor raised his eyebrows. "I sure hope you aren't here to give us bad news."

The room went silent, all eyes now on her. Realizing what he meant, Grace hurried to assure them. "No, no, she's still alive," she said. "Unfortunately, the doctors don't think she'll make it much longer. This could be her last Christmas with us."

Her voice broke on that last part, and she struggled to hold back tears. Looking around the room, she could see the sadness and concern on all their faces. These people had known Granny all their lives. Her death would be hard for them, too.

Swallowing the knot in her throat, she continued. "If this is going to be her last Christmas, I want to make it the best she's ever had."

Mayor Allen cleared his throat. "I'm very sorry to hear about Granny, as I'm sure we all are," heads nodded in agreement around the room, "And what you want to do for your granny is truly admirable. I'm not sure I understand how this fits into our town hall meeting, though?"

She took a deep breath. "Granny told me a story today about Christmas in Winterwood when she was young. I want to recreate those memories for her and need your help. All of your help," she said, looking around the room.

Bea, the owner of Bea's Bakery, patted her hand. "Honey, we would love to help you, but if you're talking about what I think you're talking about, I just don't see how it's possible,"

"I'm afraid I'm going to have to agree," Mr. Wilkins, the owner of Wilkins Five and Dime, said. "There's only twenty days till Christmas. What you're asking us to do takes months to plan."

"Not to mention the fact it takes money. Lots of money. Our little town already struggles financially," Mayor Allen said sadly. "I'm sorry, Grace, I just don't see how we could help."

"I realize what I'm asking is...ambitious," Grace said with a quick glance around the room. "But what if I told you I had a plan that would not only make this Christmas special for Granny but would also bring in a bunch of much-needed tourists and revenue? It would be a win-win."

She sighed in relief when she saw that interest had replaced the confusion and doubt on most of their faces.

"I suppose it wouldn't hurt to at least hear her out," Mayor Allen replied.

Grace beamed at him. "You all know that Granny's house is huge. I'm thinking, what if I sold all-inclusive packages for a real-life, old-fashioned Christmas to people up in the city? I bet they would pay a lot of money for the chance to unplug and return to a time when things were simpler. A time when Christmas had meaning and magic."

"I'm not sure I'm following you, dear," Bea interrupted, a frown on her face.

"I want to turn Granny's house into an inn for ten days. Bea can provide breakfast and desserts, while Addie can provide lunch and dinner at her diner. We will bring back the ice skating rink and the tree-lighting ceremony, and if we find time, we can set up a little village for Santa in the park.

"You need a business license for that," Mayor Allen said.

"I can help her with that," Katie, the town manager, said, raising her hand.

"We can't afford to be donating all that food, darlin', even if it is for a good cause," said Addie.

"Thank you, Katie," Grace replied, smiling at the woman.

She turned to Addie. "The cost of the food would be prepaid and included in the package price. I plan to rent out five rooms, so you will have guaranteed money up front for at least five people for those ten days. I would just need you and Bea to create a price list based on a family size of one, two, and four."

"I like the sound of that!" Bea exclaimed.

"I have other ideas, too. Ideas that could draw people in from the neighboring towns. People who might be willing to spend money at our stores and cafes. I know this is crazy, but we can pull this off if we work together."

"I'd be willing to offer sleigh rides," Junior Wilhelm, a farmer and Bea's husband, chimed in. "For a small fee, of course."

"I think the town still has some of its old decorations somewhere in the basement," Katie said. "I'd be willing to go down and check after the meeting."

Mayor Allen cleared his throat. "If we're going to do this, we must do it right. Tonight, I want everyone willing to participate to make a list of what you can do. We will all meet here each morning for the next two weeks to plan and coordinate our efforts. Questions?"

"What if we meet at my bakery instead? I can have coffee and doughnuts ready," Bea volunteered.

"That's wonderful, Bea, thank you. I will see all of you tomorrow morning at Bea's Bakery at eight o'clock."

"Shouldn't we discuss the regular town business before we go?" Junior asked.

"We have enough on our plate. Let's see how this goes and if it affects things for next month," Mayor Allen replied.

"I cannot thank you all enough," Grace said through tears.

Bea walked over and gave her a hug. "We all love Josephine, darlin', and you too. Let's just hope this works," she said, patting her back.

Grace smiled and gathered up her things. She intended to go down to the basement with Katie to help look for decorations and didn't want the spirited woman to take off without her. After thanking the rest of the townsfolk, she took off for the basement, a new hope springing to life in her chest.

-Days till Christmas-

Nineteen

Grace walked into Addie's diner, stunned to see that the crowd had filled the entire seating area. Spotting Bea over by the counter, she hurried over to her. "I see why the meeting was moved from your bakery to Addie's, but where did all these people come from?" she asked, her eyes wide as she looked around the room.

Bea grinned back at her. "Isn't it wonderful? We put an announcement on Winterwood's Facebook page after last night's town hall meeting, and it just blew up!"

Grace felt the tears stinging the back of her eyes. "All these people are here to help?"

Bea reached across the counter to pat her hand. "Yes, they are. Now, you better grab one of those breakfast burritos while you still can. It looks like the mayor is getting ready to start the meeting."

To her surprise, Bea pointed her toward the buffet, where she spotted several burrito trays. Addie never opened for breakfast, meaning she went to all this trouble for their first kick-off meeting. She would have to remember to give her a big hug as soon as she saw her.

Grace's ears rang from the sound of metal hitting glass. She looked up to see Mayor Allen trying to get everyone's attention. Once the room quieted down, he began to speak.

"I want to start this meeting by personally thanking each of you for taking time out of your busy schedules to be here this morning. To say that we were not expecting this many of you to show up would be an understatement, but we are so glad you came."

"I'm just here for the free breakfast!" a voice shouted from the back, eliciting a laugh from everyone in attendance.

"Regardless of why you're here," the mayor said with a chuckle, "We appreciate it." He cleared his throat and continued. "As you all know, there are only nineteen days until Christmas and only nine days until we need to turn this town into a winter wonderland. Last night, this task seemed impossible, but now, if we all work together, I think we can do it."

Cheers rang out as everyone clapped in excitement. Grace had to wipe her eyes to keep the tears from spilling over. All these people were here to help her. Their kindness and generosity were truly amazing.

Mayor Allen tapped the glass with his metal spoon again. "Because there are so many of us, I think the easiest thing to do is to break up into small groups. Someone will then assign each group a task. For example, the shop owners on Main Street will coordinate the decorating of their stores."

"I can head up a committee to get the tree for the tree lighting ceremony," Junior called out. "I just need a few strong volunteers to help me wrangle it."

"The football team can help with that," a voice from the back responded.

Grace craned her neck to see a couple of teenagers standing by the door wearing high school letterman jackets.

"We could also help get Santa's Village set up if you want us to," another teenager said.

Mayor Allen beamed at them. "That's wonderful, thank you, boys."

"I'm sure plenty of other students would help as well," Principal Adams said. "I'm willing to offer credit for community service to anyone wanting to help."

"We don't want to interrupt the kids' studies," Mayor Allen replied.

Principal Adams chuckled. "Trust me, Allen, the kids aren't counting down to Christmas. They're counting down to Christmas break. Keeping their attention this time of year is challenging at best. Besides, not all lessons can be taught from a book. Working together and getting involved with their community are valuable lessons, too."

Grace watched as everyone nodded in agreement. She pinched herself, just in case this was all a dream. Standing here, watching her friends and neighbors come together like this, felt like something out of a Hallmark movie. They hadn't even started yet, and she could already feel the magic in the air.

A lady Grace had never seen raised her hand and spoke up. "I bet the younger kids will want to be involved, too. Maybe they could help make decorations?"

"That would be great. If the teachers are willing, maybe we can task them with putting some floats together for a parade?" Mayor Allen asked.

Principal Adams nodded his head. "I'll talk to the elementary and middle school principals when I get to work this morning and get back to you with their responses ASAP."

Mayor Allen looked at his watch. "I know a lot of you need to get going, so I'll wrap this meeting up. Katie made sign-up sheets for each of the tasks we need to be done. If everyone could please sign their name on the appropriate sheet before you leave, we can get started. Grace, do you have any updates before we go?" he asked as he turned toward her.

Startled, Grace felt like a deer trapped in headlights. She cleared her throat a couple of times before she felt able to speak.

"Um, I've written an ad for the Old-Fashioned Christmas package I'm going to sell, as well as a couple of ads to post in the surrounding town's newspapers. We just need to nail down dates for the activities so I can send them out."

"I have a niece who works for a marketing agency," a lady named Mandy said from the middle of the room, her hand raised in the air. "She said she would help you advertise if you want her to?"

"That would be awesome," Grace replied enthusiastically.

"Perfect. Grace will meet with Mandy after the meeting. The rest of you, don't forget the sign-up sheets. I'll see all of you tomorrow morning, same place, same time." Mayor Allen smiled and waved as he headed for the door.

Grace hung back, waiting for the crowd to disperse. A woman, who she hoped was Mandy, approached. "Here's my niece's name and phone number," Mandy said, handing Grace a piece of paper. "She's expecting your call, so don't worry about bothering her during business hours."

"Thank you so much," Grace replied. "I was so worried about the marketing piece of this. I'm not on social media, so I have no idea how to reach out to people."

"Molly will take care of all that, don't you worry. Now, it looks like I better get over to those sign-up sheets before I get stuck following Junior on his sleigh rides and cleaning up after the horses!"

Grace laughed and watched her go. Everything was falling into place. This really was going to be the best Christmas ever.

***

Later that afternoon, Grace went into Granny's attic looking for decorations. The town wasn't the only place that needed to be turned into a Christmas wonderland. Grace had promised the house would look like a scene from a Norman Rockwell painting in the ad she and Molly had put together. She just hoped that Granny had kept the decorations from her childhood and that they were still in good shape.

She and Granny had always bought a small, live tree from the hardware store in town and used decorations they stored in the hall closet. With only the two of them, they hadn't bothered to go all out with decorations. Christmas, for them, had always been more of a reminder of the family they had lost than a celebration of what they had. It really was time for that to change. She just hoped she hadn't learned that lesson too late. It was heartbreaking to realize that she could be truly alone by this time next year.

Shaking off those depressing thoughts, she surveyed the room before her. The attic was dusty, with white sheets covering everything. All she could see was a sea of white mounds, all in varying shapes and sizes. This was going to take a while.

Starting with the mound closest to her, she lifted the sheet to discover a pile of old luggage. The next mound was hiding what looked to be boxes of encyclopedias. The next few had papers, old radios, baby clothes, and broken furniture. She hit pay dirt when she found a pair of life-size nutcrackers that appeared to still be in good condition. "These will be perfect for the porch on either side of the front door," she said out loud.

Lifting the sheets off the piles surrounding the nutcrackers, she discovered a treasure trove of Christmas decorations. There were tons and tons of lights, multiple wreaths, enough garland for the banisters and fireplace mantels, bells, Santas, and, best of all, the ornaments Granny and her siblings and cousins made when they were kids.

She had almost everything she would need to turn the house into something worthy of being on a Christmas card. The only problem was that she had to get it out of the attic and into its proper place downstairs. This was in addition to cleaning the house from top to bottom before the guests arrived. There was no way she could do it all alone, and she wondered if she could convince some of the high schoolers to help.

Just as she pulled her phone out of her back pocket to call the school, it rang, causing her to jump a few feet in the air. Her heart racing from the scare, she answered automatically without checking the caller's ID. "Hello?" she answered cautiously, figuring it was probably spam.

"Hi, my name is Hunter Parrish," the voice on the phone responded. "I'm trying to reach Grace Parker."

"This is Grace. What can I do for you?" she winced at her response. More than likely, this Hunter person was trying to reach her about her car's extended warranty. She wanted to hang up, but something kept her from doing it.

"Hi, Grace, I'm calling about your Old-Fashioned Christmas Experience."

She immediately perked up. Could this be her first guest? Already? It had only been a few hours since Molly posted about the package on her social media pages. She checked her phone and saw that he was calling from New York. So, probably not her first guest, she thought as her excitement faded.

He cleared his throat, interrupting her thoughts. "Do you still have any packages available?"

"Um, yes, yes, we do. Are you interested?" she asked, hope squeezing her chest. A part of her had been afraid that no one would book the rooms in her new pop-up inn.

"I am. The dates are December fifteenth through December twenty-sixth. Is that right?"

She nodded, even though he couldn't see her. "That's right. Will that work for you?"

"That's why I'm calling, actually. I want to book a room for those dates, but is it possible to come sooner? And stay through the New Year? My life has been very hectic lately, and the thought of unplugging and living a simpler life is really appealing to me right now."

Grace took a deep breath and let it out slowly. This was completely unexpected, and she had no idea what to do. "Uh, how much sooner are you thinking?"

"Tomorrow. If that's possible," he responded in a rush.

Grace gasped as she looked around the attic. There was absolutely no possible way they could get everything done by tomorrow. Nine days was already pushing it. However, if she said no, he would likely go somewhere else, and she would lose her first customer. She sighed in defeat. "Can I be honest with you, Hunter?"

"Of course."

"I would love to have you stay for the dates requested, but we aren't ready," she whispered.

"I didn't quite catch that last part. Did you say you won't be ready?"

"Unfortunately, yes. We just came up with this idea yesterday. The whole town is pitching in to turn this place into a winter wonderland. But we've only just started. I don't have a single decoration up, and everyone is running around like crazy, and I'm rambling. I'm so sorry." Grace bit her lip to keep from crying, surprised when she heard him chuckle.

"That sounds kind of crazy," he said, still laughing. "Can I ask what brought on this bit of madness?"

"My granny is sick. The doctors said this could be her last Christmas, and I wanted to do something special."

"I'm really sorry to hear about your granny. Is a house full of strangers really the best thing for a sick, elderly woman, though?"

She sighed. "Actually, I'm hopeful it will be the thing that saves her. She comes alive when she talks about memories from her childhood. Especially memories of Christmas. I can't help but hope that recreating those memories will breathe new life into her."

That makes sense. Even if it doesn't work, you'll still have something special to remember her by."

"Exactly," Grace said with a smile. Grateful that someone understood.

"How about this? I'll pay you the full price for the package, the full price for the days between Christmas and New Year, and half the price for tomorrow through the fourteenth. And I will help you get ready for the other guests."

"Are you serious? I can't ask you to help create the very experience you're paying me for."

"It will be a different kind of experience. I would like the chance to do something with my hands for once. Get out of this dang office and breathe some fresh air. It's completely up to you, of course."

Grace thought about his offer for a couple of minutes. She really could use some help. The money wouldn't hurt either. While she had found plenty of decorations, she still needed to buy a lot more for her guests to personalize. She was already doing something crazy. What's one more thing? "You have a deal, Mr. Parrish. Would you like me to arrange to pick you up at the airport?"

"That won't be necessary, I can rent a car. Thank you, Grace. I'm really looking forward to this. And please, call me Hunter.

"Thank you, Hunter. I'll see you tomorrow.

They said their goodbyes and hung up, the realization of what she had just done finally hitting her. He may not expect a fully decorated house, but he would definitely expect a clean room and hot meals. She was going to need those kids, and she better find Bea and Addie fast.

-Days till Christmas-

Eighteen

Grace dragged herself into Addie's for the seven o'clock planning meeting, shocked to see it was just as crowded today as yesterday. Possibly even more so. Addie really needed to charge a small admission fee to cover the cost of feeding breakfast to all these people.

Spotting Bea behind the counter again, she walked over to say hi. "Good morning, Bea, huge crowd again today."

"Good morning, darlin'. You look rough," Bea replied with a wince. "Late night?"

"A group of kids from the high school came over and helped me bring decorations down from the attic, and we managed to get a jump start on cleaning before Hunter arrives this evening. I think every muscle in my body aches right now," Grace groaned.

Bea clucked sympathetically. "I heard someone made a large pizza order at the gas station last night. That must have been you."

"Oh yeah, who knew high schoolers could eat so much! I figured feeding them was the least I could do for all their help."

"That was very sweet of you. Do you still have a lot of cleaning to do before Hunter arrives?"

Grace took a deep breath, the thought of more work causing her stiff and achy bones to groan in protest. "There's not too much left. I should be able to finish before he gets here. I feel bad, though. Everyone else is working so hard, and I'm at home cleaning. I feel like I'm not doing my part."

"Oh honey, cleaning your home is your part. You're responsible for bringing the people here. Your house is just as important as the rest of the town. After all, you're the one who will host all the guests. Have you had any more interest from prospective guests?"

"I received an email from a woman this morning. She's interested in booking a package for four. I answered some of her questions and hope to hear back from her sometime today."

"That's wonderful. Things are coming together," Bea replied, clasping her hands together in excitement. "How is Granny doing? Is she excited?"

"Granny is doing about the same, health-wise. As for the rest, I haven't told her yet. I want to decorate the house first, so I'll have something tangible to show her. She would worry I'm doing too much if I told her now."

Bea nodded. "I can see that. Surely she must have noticed all that noise you guys made last night. And how will you explain a strange man staying in the house with you?"

"I told her that a friend from high school is coming to stay for a little while and that I was having some people over to help me get ready. Granny doesn't come out of her room these days, so it's unlikely she'll notice anything until I'm ready for her."

"Sounds like you have everything under control. Looks like Allen is ready to start the meeting. Get ready for another crazy day!"

Grace turned to see Mayor Allen at the front of the room with a water glass and spoon in hand. He clinked them together a few times to get everyone's attention. "Good morning, everyone, and once again, thank you for coming. We have a lot to do, so I'll make this quick. I've spoken to Principal Adams. The high schoolers whose parents signed the permission slips will be available to help after first period. Since these are kids we're talking about, and the school will still be responsible for them, we are only allowing the seniors to help off campus during school hours. The rest will head to the elementary and middle schools to work on the parade floats."

Mayor Allen pulled a note card out of his pocket and consulted it. "Gretchen, the high school secretary, will coordinate between the high school and the committees. So, please contact her as soon as possible to request the number of students you need for your respective projects. Also, we have settled on a kick-off date of Saturday, the seventeenth, for the planned events. More details will be available in the coming days. Grace, any updates from you before we go?"

Once again caught off guard, Grace stared blankly at the mayor for a few seconds. With a quick shake to clear her head, she pulled herself together enough to give a quick response. "We already have one guest booked, which will arrive later today. I'm awaiting a response from another potential guest and will keep you updated as we go."

"That sounds great. Okay, everyone, only eight days to go until it's showtime! Things are looking great. See you all tomorrow morning."

Grace watched as Mayor Allen exited the room, his words echoing in her head: only eight days to go. She took a deep breath and looked around the room at all the excited faces. She wasn't alone, and with their help, she could do this.

Gathering her things, she marched to the door, a newfound confidence marking her stride.

***

Grace was outside untangling Christmas lights when a truck she had never seen pulled up to the curb. Curious, she watched as a handsome stranger got out and walked over to her. "Can I help you?" she called out.

When he reached her, he stuck out his hand. "You must be Grace. It's nice to meet you," he said with a smile.

Surprised, Grace shook his hand. "And you are?"

The man gave her a strange look. "Hunter Parrish. You're expecting me. Right?"

Confused, Grace checked her watch. Not only was she not expecting him for a few more hours, but the man standing before her was much younger than she had expected.

Seeing her confusion, he tried to explain. "I managed to get an earlier flight. I'm sorry I didn't let you know. In my excitement to get here, it appears I have forgotten my manners."

Grace smiled at his explanation. "Please forgive me. A lot is happening right now, and I wasn't expecting a man from New York to show up on my doorstep driving a pickup truck!"

Hunter grinned at her. "I figured, hey, when in Rome, right?"

"You think all small-town mid-westerners drive trucks?" she asked playfully.

"Yes, I do, and considering that almost every vehicle I passed on the way here was a truck, I'd say I'm right. Besides, it could come in handy if you need to pick up some large items somewhere.

"I see. So you assumed that all small-town mid-westerners had trucks except for me?" she asked in mock indignation.

He smiled sheepishly. "I wasn't sure. I figured it was best to be on the safe side. Anyway, I wanted the full country experience."

"Fair enough. How about I show you to your room? You're probably exhausted from your trip."

"That would be great. I'm looking forward to seeing the house. It's much bigger than I expected."

Grace winced. "It's kind of a mess in there. I was hoping to have a lot more done before you arrived..." she trailed off.

He smiled reassuringly and led them to the truck to get his bags. "Honestly, Grace, I'm sure things are nowhere near as bad as you think." He grabbed a couple of suitcases from the backseat of the cab. "Don't forget that I promised to help out. I'm sure between the two of us, we'll have things ship-shape in no time."

"Ship-shape?" she echoed questioningly.

"It's a term my grandpa used to say. Claimed it was from his Navy days."

"That's sweet! Speaking of grandparents, I should warn you that my granny knows nothing about all of this," she said, waving her hand toward the house. "I'm trying to keep it a surprise until everyone else arrives on the fifteenth."

"You didn't tell her I'm coming?"

"Well, yes, and no." They stopped walking, and he turned to look at her, his eyebrows raised. "I told her you're a friend from high school," Grace replied, looking down at the sidewalk in embarrassment. She hadn't realized how intimate it would feel to claim to have a relationship, even a platonic one, with a stranger. Especially when said stranger was standing right in front of her.

He surprised her when he agreed. "Hopefully, she won't grill me on our 'old' friendship,'" he replied, making air quotes with his fingers. "If there's anything I need to know about you, you better tell me now," he said with a chuckle.

"I'll give that some thought. She'll expect me to introduce you, but she pretty much keeps to herself these days. In fact, I can't remember the last time she left her room without a doctor's appointment to go to."

"It really is that bad?" he asked softly.

"I'm afraid so. That's why I wanted to do this for her. I know she'll want to come out and be involved in the festivities when everyone gets here. She needs this." Grace bit back tears, afraid of embarrassing herself again. Moving quickly, she led him up the front steps and into the house.

Thankfully, the foyer was relatively clutter-free, most of it ending up in the living room and now outside on the front lawn. She headed straight for the impressive staircase, grateful some of the girls had time to wrap the garland around the banister last night. The pretty greens and whites added some much-needed Christmas cheer.

She looked back at Hunter to see that he was gawking at the intricately carved French-style crown molding. "This is amazing," he whispered, his voice filled with awe.

"My great-great grandparents built this house. Rumor has it, they went to Paris on their honeymoon, and when they came back, they built their home styled after the French architecture they had seen there."

Hunter let out a low whistle. "This place must have cost a fortune. Even by those day's standards."

Grace shrugged. "I guess I never thought about that. This has always just been home to me. I know that my great-great grandpa was the president of the First Bank of Winterwood, so I guess he would have had a lot of money."

"If this is what the foyer looks like, I can't wait to see the rest of the house!"

Grace smiled, relieved at the semi-change in topic. "Let's start with your room. Each of the upstairs bedrooms has a small fireplace that I'm sure you'll love," she said, leading the way up the stairs and to the first bedroom on the right.

Opening the door, she signaled for him to go in while she remained standing in the doorway. In the twenty years she had lived there, except for a couple of slumber parties when she was young, they'd never had an overnight guest. These were her family's old rooms, and they'd stood empty for decades until now.

Grace wasn't sure how to feel about that. She had been so excited she had never stopped to think about the reality of opening her home to strangers. Could she really do this?

The sound of Hunter's voice interrupted her thoughts. "This room is better than anything I could have imagined. I love all the dark wood against the deep blue color of the walls. The four-poster bed is incredibly charming, and I can't wait to read a book while sitting in the wing-back chair in front of a nice, warm fire. This is perfect, Grace!"

His enthusiasm eased some of her doubt and anxiety. It was going to be okay. Besides, it's not like she's opening an actual inn. It was temporary, just for the holidays. "I'm so glad you like it. We were planning dinner around six if that works for you?"

"Sounds good to me. Is there anything you need help with in the meantime?"

"Oh no, I'm sure you would like to rest before jumping into the chaos. I'm just going to go back downstairs and finish untangling those lights."

"Are you sure? I really don't mind."

"I'm positive. There is plenty to do. You will more than earn your keep by the time we're through here," she laughed. "I'll see you at dinner."

After closing the door, she walked down the hall to her room. She hadn't checked her email in a couple of hours, and she was curious to see if anyone else had sent a response to her ad. After hitting the return key several times to wake up the computer, she logged into her email.

Besides the usual spam, she saw three messages with 'Old-Fashioned Christmas' in the subject line. The first one was from the woman she had responded to earlier that morning. She confirmed she was booking a package for a family of four and provided a rough estimate of their travel itinerary. Sure enough, when Grace checked her PayPal account, both her payment and the one from Hunter were there.

Grace shook her head in disbelief at the numbers in her account. This was really happening. She clicked back on the email tab and looked at the next message. An elderly man named Carl had recently lost his partner and didn't want to be alone for the holidays. Grace's heart broke for the man. She couldn't imagine the pain he must be feeling. Without a second's hesitation, she sent him a link to the booking page with instructions on how to pay.

The third email was from a couple with two teenage boys. According to them, the boys had grown out of Christmas, and they were hoping they could make a few more memories before the boys went off on their own. Grace's heart hurt for them, too.

Somewhere along the way, it seemed like Christmas had lost its magic for a lot of people. Sending them a link, she also felt a renewed sense of gratitude that Molly had the foresight to set up the booking process this way. It was nice to be able to choose the guests they'll be spending the holidays with. Having the ability to help even one person was gratifying.

She put the computer back to sleep. Four of the five rooms were now booked, and there were less than eight days to go until the guests arrived. She searched her desk until she found a pair of earbuds, plugged them into her phone, and chose a Christmas-themed playlist for motivation. It was time to get to work.

-Days till Christmas-

Seventeen

It had taken a long time for Grace to fall asleep last night. Hunter was a charming man, but he was still a stranger. A stranger who was staying only a few doors down the hall. It didn't take long for her imagination to run wild and convince her that every creak and moan the house made was him on his way to kill her.

Luckily, that didn't happen, or she wouldn't have been alive to answer her phone at the ridiculously early time of six-thirty. "Hello?" she answered groggily.

"Hi, Grace. It's Jenny from Bea's Bakery," a voice way too cheery for this early in the morning said in her ear. "I'm here to drop off your breakfast,"

"Oh, okay. I'll be right down." Sitting up in bed, she rubbed her eyes, then glanced around the room for her bathrobe. She was supposed to be at the diner for the daily meeting in thirty minutes. If she was going to make it on time, she would have to hustle.

She tip-toed down the hall to avoid waking her guest, then practically threw herself down the stairs as she rushed to the door. "I'm so sorry to keep you waiting," she said as she flung open the door. "I wasn't expecting you to come by today, or I would have already been out here when you arrived."

"It's okay. I hope I didn't wake everyone up when I rang the doorbell. I'm so used to being up at the crack of dawn that I forget other people are usually still asleep."

Grace winced at the thought of Granny, or worse, Hunter, getting woken up by the doorbell. She didn't want his stay to start with an unwanted wake-up call. Reaching for the bag, she thanked the woman and hurried back inside.

The scent of food wafted up from the bag as Grace rushed to the back of the house where the kitchen was. A quick peek inside revealed three styrofoam containers, each with a name, as she pulled them out individually. It was just like Bea to include her and Granny.

After grabbing three plates from the cupboard, she opened the first container to reveal a massive helping of biscuits and gravy, sausage links, and a large scoop of hash browns. A 'proper country breakfast,' she thought with a smile. Hunter was going to love this.

"Something sure smells good in here," came a voice from behind.

Grace jumped a mile in the air, her hand going to her heart. "Oh my gosh, you scared the bejeezus out of me!" she exclaimed.

"I see that," Hunter laughed. "Sorry. Didn't mean to startle you. I thought for sure you heard me come down the stairs."

"I should have, would have, if I hadn't been so focused on breakfast. Here," she said, handing him a plate. "I can throw some coffee on, or there's orange juice if you prefer?"

He looked at his watch, causing Grace to notice that he was fully dressed while she was standing there in her pajamas and bathrobe. Could this day get any worse? Oh great, she had just tempted fate by asking. Now, it was definitely going to get worse.

"Since we only have a few minutes until we need to leave, I'll settle for orange juice. Maybe we can pick up a cup of coffee in town?" he raised his eyebrows hopefully.

"Of course, Addie will probably have some at the meeting. But you don't have to go, you know. I was actually expecting you to still be asleep."

"I'm usually up by six, and since I'm still on New York time, I've been up for a little while. And I would like to go if you don't mind. I'm interested to see how this is all coming together."

"Looks like we better hurry up and eat, then. I hate to leave you alone, but I need to get Granny her breakfast and get dressed so we can go."

He smiled. "No worries. I can handle another breakfast alone." Grace could see the smile didn't quite reach his eyes. And unless she had imagined it, there was a hint of sadness in his voice. She was really going to have to do better. Her guests were paying for an experience, and eating alone in her kitchen while she rushed around was not the experience she was trying to provide.

***

They walked into the meeting just in time to see Mayor Allen clink the spoon and glass together. The diner was just as crowded as the last few days, which was a huge relief. It would have been embarrassing if Hunter had shown up to an empty place. They slowly wound their way through the crowd and over to the counter where Bea and Addie stood, a coffee pot and paper cups just off to the side of them.

As Hunter filled a cup, Mayor Allen started the meeting. "Good morning everyone. It's good to see that we haven't lost any steam yet," the mayor said as he looked around the room at all the familiar faces. "As you know, there are only seven days to go; however, I am thrilled to announce that we have made some serious progress."

The sound of thunderous applause erupted from the enthusiastic crowd. Mayor Allen waited a few moments and clinked the glass again. "Santa's Village is almost done, and the tree for the lighting ceremony is now in place. It still needs some decorations, but we believe we'll have that completed by the end of the day. Main Street is coming along nicely, and thanks to Katie, the town hall has been completely transformed. Grace?"

He looked around the room for her, and for once, Grace was ready. "I'm happy to announce that four of the five rooms have been booked," she paused while everyone cheered. "And we have just about completed the schedule for the festival. We hope to have the final details nailed down by this afternoon."

Mayor Allen nodded his head in approval. "Wonderful news. Okay, everyone, let's get to it. I'll see you all tomorrow."

Grace tried to grab Hunter and run before the rest of the folks noticed him, but she wasn't fast enough. It wasn't long before Addie's diner turned into something resembling a Luke Bryan backstage meet and greet. All the women, young and old, married and unmarried, lined up to meet the charming stranger from New York.

Taking a page from Mayor Allen's playbook, Grace picked up a spoon and glass and loudly clinked them together. When she finally had everyone's attention, she pushed her way through the crowd toward Hunter, grabbed his arm, and dragged him away. "Sorry, ladies," she called over her shoulder. "Lots of work to do. Only seven days left. You know how it is."

Once outside, they hurried over to his truck. "Thanks for rescuing me back there," Hunter said, a massive grin on his face. "I've never been mobbed by a group of women before. I feel like a movie star!"

"I can imagine," she said with a laugh. "I apologize for that. It's not every day a handsome, eligible bachelor comes to town."

He stopped to look at her. "You think I'm handsome?" he asked, batting his eyelashes.

Grace laughed despite her embarrassment. She hadn't meant to say that, at least not to him. "You know what I mean," she said bashfully.

"Where to first, madam?" he asked, seeming to take pity on her by changing the subject. Something she was extremely grateful for.

"If you don't mind, I need to make a trip up to the city to buy some Christmas trees and an assortment of ornaments."

"I thought you were planning to do a real tree? The itinerary listed a trip to a tree farm to cut down a tree, and we are all supposed to help decorate it with personalized ornaments and old-fashioned lights," he replied with a frown.

"That's correct. But that is for the tree in the living room. I want to put a tree in each one of the bedrooms and let the guests decorate them however they want. Plus, I need ornaments for the guests to personalize."

"Why not just do real trees in all the rooms?"

"I thought about that. But real trees bring with them the real possibility of a fire. I just didn't want to take the risk, especially since I'll have restricted access to the rooms while occupied."

Hunter nodded. "That makes sense. I have no clue where I'm going, so I'll need you to navigate."

Grace directed him toward Main Street, which was the fastest way out of town. Really, the only way out of town if you were going to the city. When they turned the corner, her jaw dropped open in surprise. The street had been completely transformed.

Bea's Bakery was now Mrs. Claus's Bakery, adorned with adorable gingerbread men of all sizes. Mr. Wilkins's Five and Dime was now Santa's Workshop, with toys by the dozen displayed in all the windows. Fully decorated Christmas trees lined the sidewalks while lights were strung as far as the eye could see. It was amazing.

"I take it you haven't been down here recently?" Hunter asked.

"No, why? Was it already like this yesterday?"

"Yep. It's truly something. When you told me you weren't ready, I expected to show up to a town devoid of decorations. I wasn't sure what to think when I saw this instead."

"I wasn't lying if that's what you're insinuating. Everybody has been working so hard, and with so many of us, we've accomplished much more than I thought. Everyone but me, it seems."

"Aww, don't feel bad. You've done a lot. Besides, it doesn't look like you've had anywhere near the amount of help everyone else has."

She appreciated his attempt at making her feel better, but it still stung a little. This whole thing had been her idea, and it felt like she was the only one not doing her part. Although, she supposed that wasn't entirely true. Her part just wasn't as obvious as everyone else's, at least not yet. She would feel a lot better when the house reflected all the hard work she had been doing.

Her phone rang, startling her out of her reverie. Seeing it was Molly, she answered before it could go to voice mail. "Hey Molly, what's up?"

"Hi, Grace. I hope I'm not bothering you. It's still early there. I keep forgetting I'm an hour ahead."

Grace looked at the time and saw it wasn't quite eight yet. "It's okay. I've been up for at least an hour. Besides, you could never bother me. Unless you're calling with bad news. Please don't tell me you have bad news." Grace held her breath, convinced her earlier prediction was about to come true.

"I'm not calling with bad news," Molly laughed uneasily. "I took a quick peek at the booking page and saw you still have one room available. Is that right?"

Grace released the breath she had been holding, still a little nervous about why Molly was calling. "Yes, that's correct. Is there a problem?"

"No, no problem, it's just, I was thinking..." Molly trailed off as if hesitant to finish her sentence.

Grace waited a minute to see if Molly would continue on her own. When she didn't, she tried to give her a prompt. "You're really starting to worry me now. What are you thinking?"

She heard Molly take a deep breath. "I would like to book the last room."

Grace wasn't sure she had heard her right. "I don't understand. Why is that a bad thing?"

"It's not. I just wasn't sure how you would feel about it. I know you're going for a specific vibe, and I didn't want to interfere."

"Oh, Molly, the only vibe I'm looking for is the kind where everyone feels like a big, happy family. I can definitely see you fitting into that."

Molly sighed. "Thank you, Grace. I'm going to book the room right now. I was wondering, though; I know you need help getting everything ready for the big event. Would you be willing to let me come early? I will pay you and help out as much as you need."

"How early do you want to come?"

"I already checked, and I can get a flight out of here later this morning. I should arrive sometime late this afternoon. Is that too early?"

Grace looked over at Hunter as she contemplated how two separate people made the exact same request. What was going on over on the East Coast to cause two different people to want to leave everything behind for an impromptu trip to the Midwest? "This afternoon sounds great," she finally replied. "I'll make sure your room is ready and dinner is on the table around six."

Molly breathed a sigh of relief. "Thank you, Grace. I promise you won't regret this. I love Christmas and am known around here as the decorating queen. When I'm done with it, your house will rival Lincoln Center!"

Grace chuckled. "That sounds awesome! I'm looking forward to meeting you in person. See you this afternoon."

"See ya!"

Grace pressed the end call button and turned to look at Hunter. "Looks like our party just got a little bigger."

"Another guest coming early?"

"Looks that way. Something must have happened to her. She sounded...I don't know, sad."

"This time of the year can be really hard for people. If she's sad, it's good that she's choosing to get away and surround herself with other people."

Grace nodded. She would have to remember that next year if her plan failed. "We're almost at the store. If we hurry, we can get everything we need and get home in time to clean Molly's room. We might even have enough time to get the trees up."

Hunter smiled. "We should turn this into an episode of The Amazing Race!"

"I'm not sure that's how that show worked," she laughed. "But it should. We could definitely turn this whole crazy idea of mine into a reality show!"

"Don't give them any ideas!" he grinned.

-Days till Christmas-

Sixteen

Grace returned home from the morning meeting to a completely silent house. She had invited both guests to go with her, but both had politely declined. Molly had claimed to have a bad case of jet lag and hadn't been seen since dinner the night before. Hunter said he had some work to catch up on before they started the day's tasks, but Grace suspected he wanted to avoid dealing with a repeat of the previous day. Not that she blamed him. Getting mobbed by a group of women was probably not as fun as it sounded.

Not that it really mattered. The meetings had reached a point where it took longer to get to them than to attend them, which was great when you considered the amount of work that had been accomplished in such a short time. Things were bound to get chaotic again the closer they got to the festival.

Speaking of chaos, they only had six days until the rest of the guests arrived. Six days to completely transform her mansion of a house into a cozy, Rockwell-inspired Christmas home, a home straight out of her granny's memories.

Shaking her head at the thought, a flash of color caught her eye, causing her to stop and stare at the little table in the foyer. There, right in the center, sat a little gnome. A gnome with a blue pointy hat, white beard, and blue jacket with silver snowflakes. She picked it up, briefly wondering where it had come from. With a sigh, she sat the gnome back down and continued to the kitchen.

Yesterday morning had been an eye-opener for her. Having never run an inn before, she was unprepared for the realities of hosting duties. Determined not to make that mistake again, she had made sure she was downstairs to meet Jenny at six thirty. And, before she left, she had coffee started and breakfast plated and ready to serve.

A quick peek in the kitchen showed empty plates stacked in the sink. Success? She certainly hoped so. Backing out of the kitchen, she headed to the living room, where she found Hunter and Molly talking quietly on the couch. A flash of emotion flared up in the pit of her stomach when their conversation abruptly ended the second she walked in. Was it jealousy? Yes, she had a wonderful time with Hunter, but she had only known him for a few days. Besides, these two made much more sense as a couple. They both were gorgeous, successful, career-minded people who seemed to love city life. This was real life, not a Christmas movie. In real life, people return to their lives when the vacation is over.

"Hey guys, are you ready to become decorating fiends?" she asked nonchalantly, hopeful she appeared as casual and unaffected as she was trying to be.

Molly smiled. "Of course. Just tell us where to start."

"I have exciting news. Well, hopefully, it's exciting. The meteorologist is predicting snow for the next couple of days. We should get around three to five inches. Let's start with the outside while it's still nice out and then tackle the inside while we're snowed in.

"How exciting! I hope it lasts long enough for the snowman competition," Molly replied.

"More snow is expected, so even if it doesn't, I think we'll be okay," Grace replied thoughtfully.

"Are the outside decorations ready to go, or are they stored away somewhere?" Hunter questioned.

"Most of them are already outside on the porch. I just need to grab the ladder from the garage, and we can get started."

"Sounds good. How about we all grab coats and meet on the porch in fifteen?" Molly asked as she stood up.

They all agreed and went off to get ready. Before heading back outside, Grace checked on Granny. She cracked open the door enough to peek inside and saw that Granny was still asleep, her breakfast tray untouched on the nightstand beside her. Concerned, Grace quietly closed the door. Granny had spent most of her life, as she liked to say, getting up with the roosters. The fact she was still asleep seemed like a sign she wasn't getting better, as Grace had hoped. Before the tears in her eyes could fall, she hurried outside to the garage, thankful for something to do to take her mind off Granny.

Grace walked the ladder to the front of the house where Hunter and Molly were waiting. If the three of them worked together, they could have the house decorated by lunchtime. Since the outside will be their first chance to make a good impression with the guests, she wanted it to be perfect.

"Um, what's the plan?" Hunter asked as he eyed the second story nervously.

"Don't worry, Hunter," Grace said with a laugh, "We usually just decorate the front porch."

"Thank God," he said as he let out a sigh. "That roof looks like it's over thirty feet tall."

Grace did a few calculations in her head. "That's probably about right. I plan to hang lights all along the edge of the porch and wrap garland and lights around the railings and columns. I have a lighted archway for the front of the walkway and some lighted deer to place around the yard."

Molly nodded as she looked around. "I think that sounds magical," she said somewhat wistfully.

Grace showed them where everything was, and they got to work. Hunter used the ladder to climb onto the porch roof, where he could hang the lights more efficiently. Molly focused on the railing while Grace wrapped the columns.

Grace had always loved the porch. While not a proper wrap-around porch, it ran the entire length of the front of the house and then wrapped around the sides. Which, in her mind, was close enough. The front door was right smack in the middle, a bright pop of red that stood out in contrast to the dark gray siding and bright white trim. The life-size nutcrackers gave the home a regal appearance as they stood guard on either side.

After a busy couple of hours, the three of them stood back and admired their work. It was done, and it looked beautiful. Grace wished she could bring Granny outside to see it once it got dark.

"Guess it's time for lunch," Grace said as a car pulled up in front of the house. She walked over just as Addie got out. "Surprised to see you here; the diner is usually packed this time of day."

"That's why I'm here," Addie laughed. "It's nice to take a quick break once in a while. The house looks beautiful, by the way."

Grace accepted the bag of food Addie handed her. "Thanks, Addie. For the food and the compliment."

"No problem. See you guys around dinnertime." She returned to her car and drove off, leaving the three of them standing there to admire their work again.

"Guess we should go inside before the food gets cold," Grace said as she walked toward the door.

"I wonder what we're having for lunch?" Hunter asked. "I've kind of liked not knowing what I will eat each day. It's a surprise at every meal."

"Ooh, I like that," replied Molly. "I've always loved surprises,"

"I'm sure you'll love this one," Grace grinned. "From what I can smell, it's Addie's famous pulled pork sandwiches and fries. She always includes a pickle, which I swear is the best you'll ever have."

"If it's the same recipe she used years ago, we are in for a treat!" Molly said enthusiastically. "Aunt Mandy took me there for lunch once when I was visiting, and I swear I craved those sandwiches for months! Went to every bar-b-que joint in Boston to find a substitute, but nothing ever came close. My mouth is watering at just the thought!"

"Wow! Addie should have you write an ad for her while you're here," Hunter laughed. "I'm sold and haven't even tried one yet!"

"Trust me. She doesn't need my help," Molly laughed. "Those sandwiches sell themselves."

Grace smiled at their banter. It was fun having people around. She loved being with Granny, but having people her age to talk to was nice. Maybe she would try to find some friends when the holidays were over. Join a book club or something. Even if Granny got better, she wasn't going to live forever. If Grace wasn't careful, she would end up entirely alone.

Once inside, they made their way back to the kitchen. Grace passed out the food containers and got one ready to take to Granny. Granny also loved Addie's sandwiches, so Grace was hopeful it would be enough incentive to convince her to eat. But before she got to Granny's door, it opened, surprising them all.

Everyone froze in suspense, waiting to see what happened next. Several seconds passed before Granny appeared, shuffling slowly behind her walker. Grace set her food down and hurried over. She put her arms around her to help steady her and, really, to make sure she was there to catch her in case she fell. "Here, Granny, let me help you."

Hunter jumped up as they reached the table and pulled out the chair closest to them. After getting Granny settled, Grace placed her food before her and brought her a glass of tea. "It's so good to see you up and about, Granny," Grace said as she beamed at her grandmother.

"Grace," her grandmother said, a stern expression on her face. "I didn't want to do this in front of your friends, but you've left me no choice. Whatever you're doing, you need to stop it right now."

She stared at her grandmother in shock. It had been at least a decade since Granny had used that voice with her. The last time was when she got caught watching an R-rated movie. "I-I don't understand. Stop what?"

"Gladys told me all about your ridiculous plan. I can't believe you invited strangers into my home without talking to me first. I can't believe you used my childhood memories as a reason to get them here. How could you?"

Grace's hands shook so badly the sandwich she had been holding fell on her plate. Tears stung her eyes, and she ducked her head so they wouldn't see. Taking a deep breath, she faced her granny. "I never meant to upset you. I wanted it to be a surprise. A good surprise." Grace paused to gather her thoughts. "I wanted to make our last Christmas together special."

Granny shook her head in dismay. "I know what you wanted to do. But I'm a sick old woman. Did you even once stop to consider what I might want?"

No longer capable of controlling the dam, her tears broke through and streamed freely down her cheeks. She wanted to argue, but the fact was, she hadn't stopped to think about what Granny wanted. All that mattered was getting her better. She had been incredibly selfish.

The silence was interrupted by the buzzing of her phone. Seeing it was Gretchen from the high school, she answered. After a few minutes, Grace excused herself, thankful for the reprieve. "I have to go," she announced. "There's an emergency at the school. I will talk to you when I get back," Grace called out as she hurried from the room.

Hunter and Molly exchanged glances. "Mrs. Parker, I know it's not my place, but Grace only wanted to help," Molly explained. "You mean everything to her, and she's desperate to do whatever it takes to keep you in this world."

"Yeah, well, I'm desperate to leave it."

Molly gasped. "Mrs. Parker. You can't mean that."

"It's for the best," Granny said sadly.

"But why?" Molly asked.

Granny sighed. "As you can see, my family used to have a lot of money," she said as she waved her hand around the room. "That all changed with the Great Depression. We lost almost everything when the stock market crashed. Before we had a chance to recover, World War II broke out, bringing with it sixteen years of rations, hand-me-downs, and victory gardens," Granny paused to take a drink of tea.

"We were one of the fortunate ones. Our home was paid for, so we didn't have to worry about losing it to the bank. As the oldest of my grandparents' six children, my father inherited this house when they passed. Two of his brothers died in World War I, and the remaining brothers, sisters, and their families moved in soon after the Great Depression began. I was born right in the middle of this in Nineteen Thirty-seven. Too young to have truly experienced the suffering of the times, old enough to have seen my share."

"I'm so sorry, Mrs. Parker. I can't imagine how hard that must have been for you and your family," said Molly.

Granny gave her a small smile. "We made the best of it. At one point, over twenty people lived here, at least half of them kids. It was fun having people to play with," she said with a shrug.

"I don't mean to be impatient, but I don't see a reason you should want to die," Hunter interjected.

"All the stories I told Grace about my childhood are lies. No mother who lived through the depression would ever allow her children to waste food in a food fight. If there was snow that year, we did build snowmen, but there was no tree, no hot chocolate, and certainly no ice skates to skate with."

"Why did you lie?" Molly asked gently. "Grace seems like the kind of person who would understand."

"That's precisely why I lied. She would have understood, but I didn't have the heart to tell her. That time brought with it a lot of shame and guilt. We lost everything, too, but many people judged us harshly, anyway. They thought we were unaffected by the same tragedies they were experiencing because we had this big house. Time marched on, as it always does, and those same people either moved away or passed on. At some point, life went back to normal."

Granny took another sip of tea and then clasped her hands in her lap. "Eventually, things changed, and I became the sole owner of the house. I married and had a son. Things were looking up. Then, my husband was drafted in the Vietnam War. He was a couple of years younger than me and just missed the cut-off age. He never returned, leaving me to raise my son alone."

Picking up a napkin, she wiped the tears from her eyes. "I did my best as a single mom, but it was hard. There was never enough money. Social Security only pays so much. And this house," she said, looking around. "It might be paid for, but the taxes aren't cheap. And they're due every year," she said with a sigh.

"When Grace's parents died, they didn't have life insurance. Grace received death benefits until she turned eighteen, which helped, but we still struggled. I could never give her a Christmas like the one I told her about."

"Is the problem money?" Hunter asked gently.

Granny nodded her head, her eyes glistening with tears. "I had to choose between paying the taxes on this house and buying food and my medications. This year will make three years in arrears. If I don't do something, this house will be auctioned next summer. And then we'll really lose everything." Granny choked on the last part, a sob escaping her lips.

Seeing her distress, Hunter got up and poured her a glass of water while Molly rubbed her back. "Here, try to drink some water," Hunter said, handing her the glass.

"Thank you, young man," she said as she reached out to accept it. She drank slowly, taking time to compose herself. When the water was gone, and the tears had stopped, she continued. "I didn't make the same mistake my son did. I have a life insurance policy. When I'm gone, Grace will have more than enough to take care of the house and herself for years to come."

"Are you saying you're trying to will yourself to die just so Grace can inherit some money?" Molly said, shock clear in her voice.

"It sounds a little crazy when you say it like that," she chuckled.

"Because it is crazy. Grace loves you so much," Molly explained gently. "She would be devastated if she knew what you were trying to do,"

"She convinced the entire town to put on this festival just for you. Not only does Grace love you, everyone does," Hunter added.

Granny shook her head sadly. "I know, but I must do what's best for her. She needs that money."

"Granny," Molly interrupted, laying a hand over Granny's. "After all the expenses have been paid for with the upcoming festival, there should be plenty of money left over to pay the taxes. Not only that, I think I may have a solution for your money problems. I need you to trust me for a little while as I put together a plan. Can you do that?"

"I don't know. What do you mean by trust you?"

"Try to enjoy the next couple of weeks with your granddaughter. If this does end up being your last Christmas together, don't you want it to be special?"

Granny nodded. "I'll give you a couple of weeks, but only if you promise not to say anything to Grace. If you don't end up with a Plan B, I will continue with Plan A."

"Thank you," Molly nodded in agreement. "That seems more than fair."

Granny offered her hand, and Molly shook it. The deal was official.

-Days till Christmas-

Fifteen

Grace closed her bedroom curtain and sighed. The three to five inches the meteorologist had predicted had arrived with a vengeance. And from what she could see, it would end up closer to five. The ground was piled high with snow; the streets were undrivable, and it was still coming down with no signs of stopping. Essentially, they were trapped. The one good thing about this was they canceled the morning meeting. She wasn't in any shape to face a bunch of people right now.

The emergency at the school yesterday wasn't actually an emergency. It was just an excuse she used to get out of the house as quickly as possible. Gretchen had only called to update her on the kids' progress. She would have been thrilled to hear they were almost done had her granny not just shattered her dreams only moments before.

Was she being dramatic? Probably. But she had been looking forward to recreating her granny's childhood memories with her. Christmas had always been just the two of them. They had their little tree, a couple of presents each, and a turkey and stuffing TV dinner. The memories Granny shared with her always felt like something out of a dream. A dream impossible to achieve.

People who say it's better to try and fail than to never try at all must not have ever failed. Because it sucks. Hard. She would rather have never tried than face all the people she was about to let down. She would rather have never tried than have to face her granny, who now thinks she's a selfish jerk who doesn't care about her feelings.

A quick peek at the clock on the nightstand showed it was six fifteen. Not ready to face anyone, she tiptoed downstairs to the kitchen and rushed to get the coffee started and breakfast laid out before the others woke up. Bea, always prepared, had sent over a container of assorted muffins, scones, and pastries the night before. Grace added some fruit they already had in the house, set out a couple boxes of cereal, and quickly ran back to the relative safety of her room.

Granny could not manage the stairs, and it was unlikely Molly or Hunter would bother her, so she planned to spend as much of the day in solitude as possible. Hopping back into bed, she pulled the covers up to her ears and groaned as the previous afternoon's events replayed in her head. What a mess she had made.

A flash of red caught her eye, and Grace turned to see another gnome sitting on her nightstand. This one looked like it was dressed like Santa Claus. What on earth? she thought as she reached over to pick it up. Is this a weird gnome version of Elf on a shelf? If so, who was doing it? It couldn't be Granny, and while she could see Molly or Hunter leaving a gnome in the foyer, would they really enter her room without her permission? They had been friendly, but it's not like they had known each other very long. It felt like an invasion of privacy.

Shaking her head, she sat the gnome back down and thought about the emails she would have to send that day. The two families would be upset, but they would get over it. There are lots of places they could take the kids for a vacation. Carl, on the other hand. That poor man had already experienced enough heartache. Where would he go? She had promised him a family Christmas, which wasn't as easy to find. She should look up some options for him before she emailed.

Then there were Hunter and Molly. They were already here and had spent money on plane tickets. It was bad enough she would have to refund everyone's money, especially since she had already paid a large chunk of it to Bea and Addie. Not to mention all the money she had spent on decorations. Was she going to have to reimburse their travel expenses, too? How on earth was she supposed to pay for all of this? Her side job selling digital downloads barely made enough to cover the cost of food for the month.

She could sell plasma. That was still a thing, right? Her phone rang just as her anxiety reached panic attack level. Seeing that it was Granny, she groaned and covered her head with the blanket, hoping it would drown out the sound. When the ringing ceased, she sighed in relief, only to hear it ring again. She was going to ignore it a second time, but fear that Granny could be hurt or in trouble caused her to answer. "Hello?" she said cautiously.

"Good morning, Grace. If you're up, I would like to see you in my room, please."

"I'll be right there," Grace replied as she hung up the phone. Great, she thought. Her attempts at avoiding everyone had lasted all of twenty minutes.

She put her bathrobe on, no longer concerned about the guests seeing her in her nightclothes, and made her way back downstairs. After stopping in the kitchen for Granny's breakfast, she went in to face her grandmother.

"Good morning, Grace," her granny said cheerfully. "I hope I didn't wake you?"

"Good morning," Grace replied, less than cheerfully. "I've been up for hours. Is there something I can do for you?"

"Why don't you come sit over here while we talk," Granny said, patting the bed beside her.

Grace didn't want to, but she did as she was told. The last thing she wanted was another painful confrontation.

Granny took a deep breath. "I'm sorry about what happened yesterday. I know you were only trying to do something special for me, and instead of being grateful, I was the complete opposite. I hope that in time, you will forgive me."

Grace squirmed in her seat like a little girl. "I'm the one who should be sorry, and I am. I got so caught up in trying to surprise you that I never once thought about how you would feel about the surprise. I just assumed you would be happy. Because I wanted you to be happy. It was very rude and inconsiderate of me, especially the part where I invited strangers into your home."

Granny patted her hand. "I will admit, that part was very concerning. Two single women, one elderly and disabled, alone in a house with strangers is scary. I'm sure you did your best to vet the guests you chose, but we live in a dangerous world."

"Lots of people run bed and breakfasts. Not to mention, hotels have thousands of guests a year. I figured it wouldn't be a big deal. Besides, I charged a lot of money for a particular package. I assumed that might weed out the bad actors. It appears to have worked so far."

"Ah ha! I suspected that Hunter and Molly were guests. I wracked my brain for hours, trying to remember you mentioning them while you were in school. You about had me thinking I was going senile!"

Grace laughed for the first time since their horrible exchange the previous day. "I'm sorry, Granny. You're definitely not senile. Don't worry about the guests; I will cancel all the reservations today. We will have to give Molly and Hunter a few more days due to the storm, but I'm sure they can find new arrangements by the first of next week."

"That won't be necessary, dear."

Grace frowned at her grandmother. "What do you mean?"

"I've changed my mind and want to move ahead with your plans. I don't know how much help I can be, but I would like to be involved in the rest of the decorating. Not to mention, participate in as many of the activities you have planned as possible."

Once again, tears streamed down Grace's cheeks. "Are you sure?"

Granny reached over, pulled a couple of tissues from the box on the side of her bed, and handed them to Grace. "Of course, I'm sure. What's next on the list of things to do?"

"We still need to decorate the inside of the house. We'll wait to get a tree for the living room until all the guests are here, but we need to decorate everything else."

"That sounds like fun. We can make some hot cocoa and put on some Christmas music. It will feel festive."

Grace clapped her hands together. "I already pulled all of your old decorations down from the attic. I can't wait to show you what we did outside!" she said excitedly.

A cloud passed over Granny's face. "What decorations?"

"The ones in the attic. Under the sheets?"

"I don't remember there being decorations up there."

"I'll have to show them to you, then. Surely you remember the life-size nutcrackers?"

Granny shook her head. "Maybe I'm going senile after all."

Grace laughed. "Don't be silly, Granny. It's been a long time; you probably just forgot."

"Hmm, well, we'll see. Anyway, it's time for you to get dressed. Our guests appear to be early risers, and we don't want to keep them waiting."

"Yes, Granny. I'll go change while you eat your breakfast. You need to keep your strength up."

Grace watched as Granny picked up one of the muffins. Finally convinced she was going to eat, Grace rushed upstairs to change. What a difference half an hour could make. She no longer needed to fear disappointing everyone, well, no more than usual. And she would get to have a perfect Christmas with her granny. It couldn't get any better than that.

-Days till Christmas-

Fourteen

Sunday morning dawned bright and early for Grace, who was getting used to this waking up early business. A quick peek out the window showed an expanse of snow as far as the eye could see that glistened like diamonds when the sun hit just right. It was a beautiful start to what she hoped would be another beautiful day.

The decision to cancel the daily meeting had come in via text the night before. The official reason, once again, was the weather. Since it had quit snowing around noon the previous day, and they had cleared the roads by late afternoon, she was pretty sure that was just an excuse. The more likely reason was that Sundays were the only day some committee members had off; both Bea and Addie were open every day of the week except this one. Regardless of the reason, Grace was thankful for the reprieve. Although she still had to get up to take care of breakfast for her guests.

Heading downstairs to the kitchen, she admired the decorations they had put up the previous day. The house had never looked as magical as it did right now. Twinkling lights were strung throughout, and garlands of white and green covered every fireplace mantel and stair railing. And gnomes, there seemed to be gnomes popping up in random places all over the house. Like the one that was now sitting on the counter in the kitchen. Where the heck were these guys coming from? With a shake of her head, she smiled.

After starting the coffee, Grace checked the fridge. Bea and Addie sent over large boxes of food before the storm rolled in. The packages included a combination of freshly baked goods and meals that could be reheated and ready to serve in a relatively short time. Today's breakfast was waffles, sausage, and leftover muffins from the day before. It was simple and easy for someone who never quite got the hang of cooking.

Hunter appeared right as she finished warming the sausage. "Perfect timing, as always," Grace greeted him with a smile. "Ready for breakfast?"

"I would love some," he said, returning her smile. "Sure smells good!"

"What smells good?" Molly asked as she walked in behind him. "Ooh, waffles. I love waffles!"

Grace fixed everyone a plate, took a tray to Granny, who was still asleep, and then sat at the table to eat. "Which one of you do the gnomes belong to?"

Molly and Hunter looked up from their plates and gave her a curious look. "I thought they belonged to you," Hunter replied.

"I assumed they did, too. One was sitting on the dresser in my room when I arrived the other day. I figured it was part of your Christmas décor," Molly explained.

"I had one in my room, too," Hunter said slowly. "Is this some kind of joke?"

Grace looked back and forth between them, looking for signs one or both of them were lying. After seeing none, she stared at her plate in confusion. "I swear they don't belong to me, and if they don't belong to either of you, where are they coming from?"

"Could they belong to Granny?" asked Molly hopefully.

Grace shook her head slowly. "I've never seen them before. Granny can't leave the house alone, so she couldn't have bought them. More importantly, she hasn't climbed those stairs in about five years."

"Hmm, this is quite the mystery we have on our hands," Hunter said, a thoughtful expression on his face. "Maybe we're staying in a haunted house," he said, waggling his eyebrows.

"A ghost that leaves cute little gnomes lying around?" Molly asked skeptically. "That's got to be the friendliest ghost I've ever heard of."

"Well, the ghost would have to be one of Granny and Grace's relatives, so of course, it'd be friendly!"

Grace laughed at the absurdity. "We'll have to ask Granny about it later. Maybe she does know something."

"What's on the agenda for today?" Molly asked, changing the subject.

"All that's left to do around here is clean the rest of the rooms and prepare them for the guests, but I can take care of that by myself. I still have four days until they get here."

"I don't mind helping," Molly replied. "But if we've got time, I need to do some work. Maybe we could spend the morning catching up on work and do a little cleaning after lunch?"

"That would work well for me, too. I have a long list of emails I need to respond to." Hunter agreed.

"Sounds good. I will see you guys at lunch." Grace hung back to clean the kitchen, grateful for something to occupy her time. The mystery of the gnomes was strange but seemingly harmless. What bothered her was the peculiar dynamic between this new group of people.

Molly and Hunter had only been there a few days but already felt like old friends. They were paying guests, yet they interacted with her and Granny like they were part of the family. She was confused because it had turned into a situation full of contradictions.

She might see Molly again, but only because her aunt lived there. Hunter would likely go home at the end of the month and never be seen or heard from again. How would she handle that? Would life return to normal or feel empty and hollow when they left? How will the dynamic change when the rest of the guests arrive? Will they still feel like family? Or will things become more formal?

She finished wiping down the counters and sighed. None of her questions had answers. She would simply have to continue on and let things progress naturally. She just hoped she hadn't made a mistake.

***

Granny had surprised them all by joining them for lunch again. Unlike the other day, there were no tears or accusations, just a group of people enjoying a yummy cobb salad. If nothing else, Grace would miss all the good food she had been eating lately. Not only could they not afford to eat out three meals a day, they could barely afford to eat out once a month, so they were forced to suffer through Grace's scarcely edible cooking.

After lunch, they moved to the living room to chat in front of the fireplace as Christmas classics played softly in the background. The snow, visible through the glass french doors, was the perfect touch to the cozy atmosphere.

"I hope you two don't mind an old, nosy lady, but what brought you both here?" Granny asked. She rearranged herself comfortably as if settling in for a long story. "Do you have families around here?"

Molly and Hunter were sitting next to each other on the couch. They turned to look at each other, Hunter raising his eyebrows in question. "Would you like to go first?" he asked Molly.

She shook her head. "There's not much for me to tell," she replied, squirming uncomfortably.

"That's usually a sign that you have the juiciest story," Granny said with a laugh.

Appearing to take pity on Molly, Hunter interjected. "I don't mind going first. I work on Wall Street," he explained. "I've worked hard to get where I am and am really proud of what I've accomplished, but sixty-hour-plus work weeks and non-stop stress have taken their toll," he sighed. "I'm burned out. In fact, I was just getting ready to put in my two weeks' notice when I saw the ad for Grace's Old-Fashioned Christmas Experience and decided on the spot to give it a try and put in for vacation instead."

Granny nodded her head knowingly. "Even when you're young and like what you're doing, that kind of pressure has a way of getting to you."

Hunter nodded. "As for family, my sister and brother-in-law moved to Scotland a couple of years ago so she could complete her doctorate degree. She just had her first baby, so naturally, my parents have practically moved there to help out. Baby's first Christmas, you know!"

"How sweet. You didn't want to go too?" Granny asked.

"It's not that I didn't want to go. I feared it would change the dynamic if I showed up. My parents are there to help out. If I went, my sister would feel compelled to play hostess and insist on entertaining me instead of getting the rest she needs."

"I can certainly understand that," Granny nodded. "It's very kind of you to recognize that and even kinder to put your sister's needs first, even though it's costing you the chance to spend the holidays with family."

Hunter gave her a big smile. "I may not be spending the holidays with my family, but I am still spending them with family. Besides, if my sister makes her stay in Scotland permanent, I feel my parents will officially move there, too, something I will need to get used to."

"You don't think they'd want to stick around to see you too?" Molly asked in surprise. "After all, you may have kids yourself someday."

"I'm sure they would want to be around if that happened, but since I'm not even dating someone, much less anywhere close to marriage, I can't see them giving up a chance to spend time with their actual grandchild in favor of one that may never exist. If that should happen someday, I imagine they'll go back and forth."

"Makes sense. What about you, Molly?" asked Granny.

All eyes were now on Molly. She sat quietly while Hunter talked, hoping they would forget about her. After taking a couple of moments to visibly compose herself, she finally spoke.

"I'm not sure if you know this, Granny, but I'm the one who helped Grace put together the marketing material for the experience packages she sold. We spent hours discussing the town, the events that will take place, and the experience she wants the guests to have overall. After all that, I just wanted to join the fun."

She stopped talking for a minute, the room silent as everyone looked at her. As if sensing her explanation wasn't enough, she continued. "I knew how much work Grace was going to have ahead of her if she was going to get ready in time, so I thought if I came early, I could help her out."

"You were willing to do that for someone you hardly knew?" asked Granny.

"Aunt Mandy told me the real reason Grace was doing all this. So yes, I was willing to do whatever I could to help," Molly responded, looking at Granny pointedly.

Grace watched their exchange, confused by the unspoken communication. Why did it always seem like something was going on that she was unaware of? Were these people holding secret meetings she wasn't invited to?

Molly interrupted her thoughts by asking her a question. "What about you, Grace? What's your story?"

Surprised, she stared into space for a few minutes, looking for an answer that wasn't embarrassing. Compared to the two of them, she had very little to show for her life. "I'm not sure what to say. I went to college for a couple of years, then dropped out and moved back home after Granny fell and broke her hip. I've been here ever since, acting as her full-time caretaker."

"Do you work at all?" Molly asked gently.

Grace took a deep breath and let it out slowly. "Granny needs someone here at all times, so I can't work outside the house. Several years ago, I read an article about a woman who created and sold printables as a side hustle. It sounded interesting, so I decided to try it too. It's not making me rich, but I earn enough to help with food and some bills."

"That sounds pretty cool," Molly enthusiastically replied. "I buy printables all the time. I might have even bought some of yours without knowing it!"

Grace smiled gratefully at Molly. It was very kind of her to make Grace feel better about herself. Not that there was anything wrong with her, per se; it was just hard not to compare herself to these two and not find herself lacking. Except for those two years at college, which was only thirty minutes away, she had never lived outside her small town nor pursued a career. She hadn't even officially declared a major when she was forced to drop out. Her life just felt so small...and bland.

"Well, I have enjoyed talking to all of you, but I think it's time for my afternoon nap," Granny said, interrupting Grace's thoughts.

Grace jumped up to help Granny to her room. After she was settled, Grace returned to the living room, where Molly and Hunter were still seated.

Pasting a big smile on her face, Molly turned to look at Grace. "How about we get started on those rooms upstairs?"

"No, seriously, you don't have to help with that," Grace replied, holding her hands out as if to stop her. "I've got it under control."

"I do believe that I promised to help as part of the agreement for me to come early..."

"I also promised, if memory serves me correctly," Hunter interrupted.

"Besides, it will be more fun if we all help," said Molly. "We can put on some upbeat Christmas music and have it knocked out in no time."

"Plus, we might find a clue to the gnome mystery," Hunter said in a spooky voice.

Grace laughed. "Okay, you convinced me. Thanks, guys; having you around will be more fun."

"Let's go," Molly said, jumping off the couch and looping her arm through Grace's.

Hunter got up, looped his arm through Grace's other one, and they headed upstairs together.

-Days till Christmas-

Thirteen

Only three more days until the guests arrived and the festivities began. Grace was both excited and nervous. She had gotten the hang of providing food and drinks throughout the day and was eternally grateful for the practice run Hunter and Molly had given her, but they were two very laid-back people. Nine more people were coming, which meant nine times the amount of food, nine times the amount of drinks, and likely nine times the amount of chaos.

Then there was the cleaning. She had only factored in cleaning the rooms before everyone arrived, completely blanking on the fact that eleven people would be staying for at least eleven days. Her days as a maid were just beginning. Bea was right; she had a lot to do. If she ever decided to do this again, she would have to sit down and think about all the time she spent caring for guests when she put together her prices. That was a big IF.

As Grace scrubbed the toilet, one of her least favorite chores, she tried to remind herself why she was doing this in the first place. As far as she could tell, her plan was working. Granny had come out of her room to have lunch with everyone every day for the last three days. That was more than she had done in the last three months. Her spirits also appeared to have improved dramatically. Even Gladys had commented on the improvements when she left after Wheel of Fortune last night. That was definitely worth having to clean a few bathrooms.

The doorbell rang just as she was finishing up, which was perfect timing on her part. Lunch had just arrived. Hurrying quickly down the stairs, she got to the door just as the doorbell sounded a second time. At least she was getting a good workout. This was the most active she'd been in months. She swung open the door to greet Addie, only to find Gladys instead. "Hi, Gladys. You're a little early for the 'Wheel,' aren't you?"

Gladys handed her a large bag that smelled suspiciously like tuna. "I was going crazy being cooped up in that big house by myself. I went down to Addie's for lunch, and when I saw her bagging up your order, I got mine to go and decided to join you for lunch. I do hope you don't mind."

"Of course not. You're welcome anytime. Hopefully, you know that," Grace replied, hugging the older woman. "Come on in. I bet everyone else is already waiting for us at the table."

Grace led the way down the hall to the large dining room/kitchen combo. It had always been her favorite room in the house. A fireplace sat in the corner, lending an air of coziness on cold winter days. A brass chandelier, the size of a small bear cub, hung above a table that could easily seat twenty. The table itself, built around the same time as the house, offered a tiny glimpse into the lives of generations past. Grace could almost picture her granny as a little girl sitting at the big table surrounded by family.

When they entered the room, three smiling faces greeted them. "Lunch has arrived," Grace announced as she set the bag on the table. "Hope everyone likes tuna!"

They took turns greeting Gladys as Grace passed out styrofoam containers of pickles, potato chips, and tuna salad on a lightly buttered brioche bun. Grace was definitely going to miss this when it was back to peanut butter and jelly every day.

Granny and Gladys regaled them with tales of their nightly game show contests, eliciting bursts of laughter from Molly and Hunter, but Grace couldn't concentrate, her mind continuously wandering off. For years, she had been content to float along with no real purpose beyond caring for Granny. She would happily continue doing so for as long as Granny was with her, but what happens after that? Once Granny passed, be it this year, the next, or even ten years from now, Grace would be alone in this big wide world; her only purpose would be gone. Heavy thoughts for such a lighthearted mood.

The doorbell rang, and she excused herself to answer it, curious who it could be. She opened the door to reveal a tall, dark-haired man wearing what looked like very expensive, tailored winter clothes. Hoping this wasn't another guest arriving early, she greeted the stranger. "Hi, can I help you?"

"Um, I hope so. I'm looking for Molly Hawthorne. Is she here, by any chance?"

The man had a strong Boston accent, not unlike Molly herself. "May I ask who's inquiring?"

The man reached out his hand. "I'm Grant Hawthorne, Molly's husband."

Grace's eyes went wide. Molly's husband? She never said she had a husband. Momentarily forgetting her manners, Grace winced as she noticed the man's waiting hand. Quickly reaching out to shake it, she tried to think of what to say. She couldn't leave the man standing on her porch in the cold, but what if she brought him inside and he became a threat?

"Grace? Is everything okay?" Molly asked from the hallway behind her.

Grace turned to look at her. "There's someone here to see you," Grace replied nervously.

Molly laughed. "Well, who is it? Is it Aunt Mandy?"

Grace shook her head and stepped away from the door, giving Molly a clear view of the porch. She gasped when she saw who was standing there.

"Oh my gosh, Grant. What are you doing here?" she exclaimed.

Grant looked from Molly to Grace and then back to Molly. "Can we talk? Please," he asked quietly.

Molly shook her head. "I've already said everything I have to say."

"That may be true, but you never allowed me to say what I need to say."

"I just— It's too painful." Molly turned and hurried away, back toward the dining room. Grant watched her for a moment before rushing past Grace and following.

After closing the door, Grace ran after them, hopeful one of the others would know what to do. When she reached the dining room, she saw that Grant and Molly stood in front of the fireplace, all eyes on them.

"Come on, Molly," Grant pleaded with his wife. "You can't throw away ten years of our lives without at least giving me a chance to work this out. That's not fair."

"I've given you more than a dozen chances. It's not my fault you waited until I had finally given up to take things seriously," Molly said, her voice rising angrily. "Admit it. If I hadn't left, everything would still be the same, wouldn't it?"

Grant shook his head. "You're wrong, Molly. I know I should have talked to you sooner, but I wanted to make sure I could do what you asked before I made promises I couldn't keep. Things have changed, I swear."

"Oh yeah, like what? What's changed, Grant?"

"For starters, I quit my job."

Molly's head reared back as if she had been slapped. Her anger quickly turned to shock. Shaking her head, she stared at him, her mouth opening and closing, yet no words came out.

Grant reached out his hand, letting it drop back to his side when she stepped back. "I'm serious, Molly. I handed in my two weeks last Monday. I was going to tell you, but then we had that fight. You were so mad I thought it would be better to give you a couple of days to cool off first, but when I came home Wednesday night, you were gone." Grant shook his head sadly. "It took me days to figure out where you went. I booked the first plane I could when I found out."

"I don't know what to say. I was so sure that nothing would ever change I accepted it was over. How do we move forward from that? Is it even possible?" Molly whispered, tears streaming down her cheeks.

"All I know is that I love you, and if you still love me, then anything is possible. We just need some time to find our way back to each other." Grant turned to look at Grace. "Do you have any more rooms available? I would like to be near my wife, but she may need some space for a while."

"I-I'm sorry, but we're all booked up," Grace replied apologetically.

"I have a room you can rent," Gladys interjected. "Things aren't quite as festive at my place, but it's right next door. Other than that, I'm afraid your options are limited to renting a hotel room in the city," Gladys said with a shrug.

"I will happily accept your gracious offer. Thank you, Ms.?" he asked questioningly.

"You can call me Gladys," she replied as she got up. "How about we go next door and get you settled? I think Molly could use a little of that space right about now."

"That sounds great." He turned to face Molly. "Can we talk later? Maybe at dinner?"

"We usually have dinner here," Molly replied absent-mindedly. "Not a lot of privacy."

"How about I call you in a few hours? See how you're feeling?" he asked hopefully.

Molly nodded.

Grant turned back to the rest of the group. "It was nice to meet all of you. Ms. Gladys, I'm ready if you are."

Gladys led him out of the room. The rest looked at each other, unsure what to say or do. After a few minutes of silence, Molly returned to the table and sat down. "I guess I owe you guys an apology," she said softly.

"An apology for what, dear?" Granny asked.

"I lied to you. I told you I didn't have a family. In my defense, I truly believed it was over between Grant and me."

"You don't owe us an explanation, Molly," said Hunter. "Your marriage is your business. I can only imagine how painful these last several days have been for you."

"If you want to talk about it, we're here," Granny said, patting her hand. "Sometimes, talking to strangers is actually easier. Helps to get an unbiased perspective."

Molly sighed. "Maybe you're right. Grant and I have been married for ten years and together for twelve. We met in our senior year of college, back when the world seemed full of possibilities," she said with a wistful smile. "The world was our oyster; we were convinced we could have it all."

She shook her head sadly. "Somewhere along the way, we got lost. Our careers became our primary focus. Talks of buying a home, settling down, and having kids became few and far between. I was happy to accept it for a while; after all, I was focused on my career, too. But these last couple of years, things changed for me."

Molly paused to gather her thoughts, pain clearly written on her face. "I woke up one day and heard my biological clock ticking loudly in my ears, so to speak. I know that women are having kids well into their forties these days, but even with modern medicine, the risks are still there, not to mention the increased risk of infertility. I felt in my heart that the window was closing."

"What happened last week?" Granny asked gently.

"A co-worker of mine announced her pregnancy. That same day, Grace called and asked for my help with the

Old-Fashioned Christmas Experience," Molly said, turning to look at Grace.

"I caused you to feel bad?" Grace asked, completely horrified at the thought.

"No, no, of course not. It was the pictures of all the smiling, happy families celebrating Christmas together. I realized that if I didn't do something drastic soon, I would never have that. I couldn't handle missing out on something so important to me for the rest of my life. So, when Grant came home, I asked him again if we could talk about our plans for a family. I lost it when he asked me if we could wait and talk about it in a couple of weeks." Molly shook her head. "I was done."

"That's when you decided to come here?" asked Grace.

Molly nodded. "I saw you still had a room available, so I called you to ask about it. I figured this would be the perfect place to come and lick my wounds," she said with a smile. "I hoped I would be so busy I wouldn't have time to think about everything."

"What are you going to do now?" asked Grace.

"I honestly don't know."

"It's not really my business, but if Grant quit last Monday, it sounds like he is dedicated to making changes," said Hunter. "It might be worth it to at least hear him out."

"You're right. Even if he didn't quit, coming here is a sign he's willing to at least do something. He never would have missed work in the past, especially not on a Monday."

"How about this?" asked Granny. "Grace can take Hunter out for dinner tonight. They can drive around looking at lights when they're done. I will stay in my room, and you and Grant can have the dining room. That way, you can have plenty of privacy. How's that sound?"

"We couldn't possibly put you guys out like that," said Molly. "Grant and I can go somewhere."

"I know I don't mind, and I'm sure Grace doesn't either," said Hunter. "A restaurant is no place for the conversation you need to have."

Molly nodded. "If you're sure?"

Everyone nodded their heads.

"Thank you. I will pay for your dinner since you guys are going out," Molly offered.

"There's no need," Grace assured her. "We can just go to Addie's; it's already taken care of that way."

"Okay then, I guess it's settled. If you guys don't mind, I think I will go upstairs and lie down for a little while before I call Grant." Molly got up and left the room after assurances from the rest of them.

Granny stood up to return to her room. I'm going to need a nap as well. See you kids later," she said with a wink.

Grace looked at Hunter. "Guess I better get some work done before it's time to go."

"Hey, how about we go back to the city instead?" Hunter asked. "I saw a cute little Italian restaurant last time we were there. It will take more time, and I bet there's a lot more lights to see."

Surprised by his offer, Grace took a minute to respond. "That sounds great. I'll let Addie know that our plans have changed."

Hunter gave her a big smile. "Awesome! It's a date; I'll drive!"

Grace laughed nervously. Did he mean an actual date? Or was it just an expression? "Any excuse to drive your truck, eh?"

"You know me too well!"

Did she? Just what she needed. A bunch of cryptic sayings she had no experience trying to figure out. What did one wear on a date that might not be a date? Heck, what did one wear on a date that was a date? She really needed to get out more. Hunter was way out of her league, and it was only a matter of time before she embarrassed herself beyond the point of no return.

-Days till Christmas-

Twelve

The sound of the alarm clock ringing woke Grace from a deep sleep. Groaning, she reached over to turn it off, so much for getting used to waking up early. Although, in her defense, she went to bed later than usual the night before.

Her 'date' with Hunter had been fantastic. First, they went to Bella's, an adorable Italian restaurant with the most romantic atmosphere. There were no tables, only booths with tall backs, lending an air of privacy and seclusion to the dining experience. The lights were dimmed, the primary light source coming from the candles on the tables, making it an authentic candlelight dinner.

While a part of her recognized it was unlikely Hunter knew about this beforehand, the other part wanted to believe his choice of restaurant had been intentional. They had spent hours talking about everything and nothing, and she was sure she had never laughed more in her entire life than she did last night. When they were done, they drove down to the shopping district and walked around arm in arm, looking at the lights and window displays. It had felt magical and exciting and, well, perfect.

Grace sighed at the memory. She had gone on a couple of dates, but those had either consisted of dinner at Addie's or a group outing to the rodeo. Not to mention the fact they happened when she was in high school over five years ago. There just weren't any single men her age living in Winterwood. Most of the guys she went to school with moved away long ago. The few that stayed were already married with children of their own.

That's not to say that last night was an actual date. It likely wasn't, and she knew that. Hunter never indicated last night was anything more than two friends hanging out together. Well, other than when he jokingly called it a date. A girl can still dream, though, can't she? If nothing else, last night was a vivid reminder that she needed to get out more. She would love to get married and have a family someday, which would never happen if she stayed cooped up in the house all the time.

She finally dragged herself out of bed and dressed, carefully watching the time. There had been no sign of either Molly or Grant when they got home last night, and Grace wanted to get downstairs before the doorbell rang, just in case Molly needed extra rest. Although she was really curious about how things had gone the previous night. Her romantic side hoped love would conquer all and Molly and Grant would get their happily ever after.

At six twenty-five, she stepped onto the porch to wait for Jenny, immediately regretting not dressing warmer. Overnight temps were in the low twenties, and the ground was still covered in snow. Thankfully, a car pulled up not even a minute later. Grateful she had taken the time to shovel the walkway the day before, she rushed down the steps to meet Jenny at her car.

After a quick greeting, she grabbed the bag of food and rushed back inside. They were starting the daily meetings again, and Grace needed to get breakfast ready before she left. She quickly got a fire going in the dining room fireplace, started the coffee, and set out plates and silverware. Today's breakfast was french toast, sausage, bacon, and scrambled eggs. When she opened the containers, the smell of cinnamon permeated the air, giving the room a decidedly Christmas feel. Which reminded her she needed to look up a recipe for mulled cider; nothing screamed Christmas like mulled cider.

She arranged a tray for Granny, put her guest's plates on the warming tray, and then scarfed her food down as quickly as possible. She was out the door and down to Addie's with only minutes to spare. It'll be nice when these meetings are no longer required; rushing around each morning is not fun.

Grace made it inside just as the glass clinked, signaling the start of the meeting. "Good morning, everyone; thank you for coming. I hope you all have been staying warm," Mayor Allen said, smiling warmly at everyone. "I know we need to make this quick, so I'm going to turn the meeting over to Grace so we can get going. Grace?" Mayor Allen searched the room for her.

Surprised again, Grace headed to the front of the room. It would be nice if he would warn her before doing things like this. She had not been prepared to lead the meeting this morning. Turning to face the crowd, she took a deep breath and smiled at everyone. "Good morning. I just want to say thank you to everyone for all of your hard work.

The town looks beautiful, and I know all our out-of-town visitors will love it!"

Everyone clapped and cheered, including Grace. When they settled down, she continued. "We will kick off the Christmas festival this Saturday around ten o'clock. Vendors from both in-town and out-of-town will set up booths around the park, activities for the kids, and a couple of adult competitions. At five thirty, the parade will start at the high school, travel down Main Street, and end at the park, just in time for the tree lighting ceremony."

She took a deep breath as she thought about the itinerary. "And, following that, there will be a concert in the park. Several hot cocoa stations will be set up throughout, along with strategically placed fire-pits to help keep everyone warm. Questions?"

"Who will be in charge of the fire-pits?" a lady in the front row asked. "We don't want anyone getting hurt."

Grace nodded. "Volunteers from the fire department will man the fire pits. We also have a couple of police officers from the surrounding towns coming by to patrol. So we should have plenty of help available in case there's an emergency."

The lady nodded, appearing satisfied by Grace's answer. "Anyone else have questions?" Grace asked as she searched the crowd.

"What kind of advertising have you done?" asked a man from the back.

"We've been running daily ads in the newspapers of all the surrounding towns and the one up in the city. We have also been posting on social media and have a contest running where every time a person likes our posts, they are automatically entered into a drawing for some great prizes sponsored by our local businesses."

Grace looked around the room to see if anyone else had more questions. When the room stayed silent, she looked to Mayor Allen to end the meeting. "All of that sounds great!" he said enthusiastically. "I would appreciate it if everyone checked in with their committee leaders before they left. There is still some work to be done. Thanks, everyone, I'll see you tomorrow."

Mayor Allen headed toward the door, Grace hot on his heels. When they reached the parking lot, he turned to look at her. "Did you need something?"

She shook her head. "No, sir, I just needed to get out of there, and following you seemed to be the fastest way to do it."

Mayor Allen chuckled. "I do seem to have a way of clearing a path. Good work, Grace; I look forward to seeing how this works out."

"Thank you, sir. I do, too. Hopefully, it works out well for both of us."

They parted ways, Grace anxious to get home. There was still work to be done at the house, and there were only two days left before the rest of the guests arrived. Not to mention, she needed to prepare for Christmas itself. Bea and Addie would provide food in advance, which would help, but Grace had volunteered to cook Christmas dinner so they could focus on their families. Why she had done that was anyone's guess. She couldn't cook to save her life, and now she would cook for thirteen. She clearly needed to have her head examined. Now, she had recipes to test and grocery shopping to add to her to-do list.

As she pulled into the driveway at the back of the house, she saw Grant and Molly make their way through the bushes separating Granny's yard from Gladys's. At first, it looked like a couple of teenagers sneaking home after staying out all night, but as they got closer, Grace could see that Grant was struggling to carry a large box while Molly kept looking behind her as if to make sure something was still there.

Hurrying over to see what was happening, Grace finally spotted what Molly was looking at: a medium-sized brown and white dog following warily behind them. "What on earth!" exclaimed Grace.

"We need to get them inside before they freeze to death. Grace, I know this is a lot to ask, but do you mind?" asked Molly, her face full of concern.

"Of course not. Let's go in the back door," Grace replied, unlocking the door. "Take them into the dining room in front of the fireplace. I'll be right back with some blankets."

Grace hurried off to the upstairs closet and grabbed a handful of regular and heated blankets. Hunter opened his door as she turned to head back down and popped his head out. "Everything okay?" he asked.

"I don't know. We have a situation downstairs. I need to get down there," she replied over her shoulder as she hurried back down.

Hunter followed, and they burst into the room just in time to see half a dozen puppies climb over the side of the box Grant had been carrying.

"Oh my gosh!" Grace exclaimed. "Where did these guys come from?"

Molly shook her head. "We're not sure. Grant and I decided to go for a walk this morning, and when we got back, we heard this horrible whimpering sound. After walking around the property a few times, we finally found the mama dog and her puppies hiding in one of the window wells by the back door."

Grace and Molly made a blanket nest in the front of the fireplace while Hunter grabbed some bowls of water from the kitchen, and Grant attempted to corral the puppies. When the dogs were finally settled, Grace searched the room for her phone. "We need to get them to the vet as soon as possible. Who knows how long they've been out there?"

"I'm sure they belong to someone local," said Grant. "They probably escaped this morning as someone left for work. Right?" he asked hopefully.

Grace looked at him sadly. "The country tends to be a dumping ground for people who no longer want their pets. I would be willing to bet a lot of money the owner of this dog decided he no longer wanted to deal with her and her puppies, so he dropped her off in the middle of the night last night."

Molly gasped in shock. "It was freezing last night. Surely no one could be that cruel."

Grace shook her head. "It wouldn't be the first time. I'm just glad you guys found them so soon. Gladys rarely uses her back door. If you hadn't found them..." she trailed off, the rest of her sentence too hard to say out loud.

Grace called the vet clinic and explained the situation; Hailey, the veterinarian, graciously agreed to make a house call so mama and babies wouldn't have to endure the additional trauma of being moved again.

While Hunter, Grant, and Molly took turns petting the mama and playing with the puppies, Grace got a sheet of paper and a pen to make a list.

"What are you doing?" asked Molly as she looked up at her from the floor.

"I'm making a list," Grace replied absentmindedly.

"A list for what?"

"Dog supplies. We will need food, toys, beds, collars, leashes, and whatever else Hailey recommends. This reminds me, I better check with the other guests to make sure no one has any pet allergies. I'm assuming none of you are allergic to dogs?" she asked, looking at each of them for a response.

When they all shook their heads no, she nodded and continued writing.

"You're going to keep the dogs? All the dogs?" asked Hunter.

Grace shrugged. "Where else are they going to go? The puppies don't look big enough to leave their mama yet, so finding them homes is out of the question. Shelters are already bursting at the seams, and I sure as heck ain't sending them back outside. That leaves only one option."

Hunter grinned up at her. "I have a feeling this Christmas just got a whole lot crazier."

Grace smiled back. "I think you meant to say cuter. Christmas just got a whole lot cuter!"

-Days till Christmas-

Eleven

Wednesday morning came way too early for Grace. Hailey, the local veterinarian, had stopped by the day before and, after a thorough examination, had given both mama and babies a clean bill of health. The puppies were estimated to be approximately five weeks old, old enough to run around and play but too young to leave mama. Grace volunteered to foster them until the puppies were old enough to be adopted.

After moving them all to the more comfortable and easier-to-contain area in front of the living room fireplace, the puppies had spent the day comfortably snuggled up together. It had been adorable. What had not been adorable was when they woke up, sometime around eleven o'clock, wanting to play, and play they did. Grace had ended up sleeping on the couch to keep an eye on them, hence her nearly sleepless night. This must be what people meant when they say dogs prepare you for babies.

Stretching her arms and legs while she yawned, she headed toward the front door; it was time for the breakfast delivery. After her usual exchange with Jenny, she went to the kitchen, desperate for coffee; it was going to be a long day. Thankfully, all that was left to do upstairs was put fresh linens on the beds. She was sure she could handle that, even in her tired state.

What she didn't think she could handle was another morning of rushing around to get to the meeting. A quick series of texts later, and Bea had agreed to cover for her. Grateful that was settled, she set about preparing breakfast. Could she do this every day? She had been toying with the idea of opening up a permanent bed-and-breakfast. If everything went according to plan, they would make a lot of money on this go around. It was a lot of work, but not having to worry about how to pay the bills held a lot of appeal.

Shaking her head, she dismissed the idea. They lived in the middle of nowhere. The town had exactly zero tourist attractions, and she had a sick granny who needed full-time care. A full-time bed-and-breakfast had no chance of success. She would just have to find another way to make money.

Not long after Grace sat down to eat, Molly appeared in the doorway. "Good morning," she sing-songed, looking happier than Grace had ever seen her.

"Wow, you're in a good mood. Things must be going well with Grant?" asked Grace. "Not that I'm trying to be nosy or anything."

Molly laughed. "We've been having a great time together. Better than we've had in a long time. Living separately has made us feel like we're dating again. It's exciting!"

Grace nodded as she turned her attention back to her plate. She was happy for Molly; she really was. But she was also jealous. A feeling she was experiencing all too often these days. A feeling that she was deeply ashamed of. It wasn't Molly's fault that Grace kept comparing herself to her. Molly deserved every good thing that came her way. She had worked hard to earn it. If Grace decided she wanted that, too, she would also need to work hard.

"How are our new guests doing this morning?" asked Molly cheerfully.

Grace's head shot up in surprise. "New guests? What new guests? Did someone else arrive early?" she asked in a panic.

Molly reached out to pat her hand. "Calm down, Grace. No one else has arrived. I was referring to the puppies."

"Oh. Okay, good. The puppies are fine."

"You look exhausted. Are you feeling okay?" asked Molly, concern evident in her voice.

Grace shook her head. "I'm fine. I was just up half the night with the puppies. They woke up wanting to play and kept finding ways to escape the makeshift pen," she yawned.

"Why don't you go upstairs and take a nap? Grant will be over soon, and we can take over puppy-sitting duties."

"That sounds great, but I have so much to do. I still need to go to the store, so there isn't time for a nap."

"Nonsense, it's still early. There's plenty of time for trips to the store later. Besides, you're too tired to even make a list right now."

"I already have a list. I made it last night," Grace said, pointing to the paper on the counter.

"In that case, you're too tired to be driving. I'm serious, Grace; you need to rest. It's only going to get more chaotic from here."

Grace nodded. "Thanks, Molly, I appreciate all your help."

Molly smiled. "Happy to do it."

Grace took one last peek at the puppies before dragging herself to bed. They really were adorable when they were asleep. She passed Hunter in the hallway but barely had enough energy to grumble a good morning. She would need to remember to apologize the next time she saw him. Some host she was.

***

After a few hours of sleep and a hot shower, Grace felt almost human again. She went downstairs and headed straight to the living room to relieve Molly and Grant, only to find Hunter instead. Grace stood in the doorway momentarily, taking in the adorable scene before her. Hunter sat on the floor, his back resting against the couch. Mama was curled beside him, resting her head on his thigh, while the puppies were jumping over his legs and wrestling with his feet. He had become a puppy jungle gym, and judging by his smile, he loved every minute of it.

Worried he'd catch her staring, she walked into the room. "Where's Molly and Grant?" she asked, smiling when two puppies slid across the hardwood floors to get to her.

"They went to the store. Said to tell you they had some shopping they wanted to do, so they took your list too, and not to worry about it."

"Oh, that was really kind of them," Grace replied, relieved she had one less thing to do yet concerned she was pawning her tasks off on her guests. That was definitely not good host behavior, according to the hundred or so articles she had read on hosting in the last couple of weeks.

Hunter watched her face, his eyes narrowing slightly. "Molly was happy to help, Grace. Don't feel bad about accepting help when you need it, especially when the very people offering to help are the ones you made an agreement with for that very thing."

Grace shook her head. "I know, it's just..." she trailed off, unsure what to say. How did she explain how she felt when she wasn't even sure herself?

Hunter patted the floor beside him. "Come sit down with me."

Grace's eyes opened wide in surprise, but she did as she was told. The puppies immediately surrounded her, excited for new smells and a new person to play on. Laughing, she tried to pet them all.

Hunter waited until the puppies settled a bit before he spoke again. "You've been taking care of your granny for a long time. By yourself, I take it?" He waited for her to nod before continuing. "You've conditioned yourself to do everything alone, not asking for help, even when needed. I don't blame you; I think that's something most people struggle with in your position. But you need to realize that letting people help you is okay."

"I know," she replied softly. "But I'm supposed to be doing these things. You guys are paying me to be here. It's my job. Literally."

"Have you forgotten the agreement you made with me and Molly?" he asked, turning her face to look at him. "The agreement was that we came early in exchange for helping you get ready. You did your part. You need to allow us to do ours."

Grace blinked back tears. "You make it sound so simple, and I guess it is, but it just doesn't feel that way for some reason."

"I know; that's the part you need to work on. You're a young woman with her whole life ahead of her. What you're doing for your granny is honorable—"

"It's no less than what she did for me," Grace interrupted.

Hunter sighed. "You don't have to defend yourself to me; I'm just trying to tell you it's okay to accept help. It's okay to have a life of your own. You don't have to be everyone's caretaker, at least not all the time."

Grace thought about what he said. It was difficult to hear, but deep down, she knew she needed to. "Thanks, Hunter, I appreciate it."

"You're welcome. Now, there's something important we need to do."

"Oh. What's that?" she asked curiously.

"These guys need a name," he replied, picking one of them up to cradle in his arms. "There's going to be a lot of people coming tomorrow, and they're not going to be able to resist all this cuteness!"

Grace watched him laugh as the puppy licked his face and wished with all her heart she could freeze this moment in time. Apparently, all a man had to do to win her heart was play with a puppy. Although, if she was being honest, she had developed a crush on him long before the puppies had shown up.

"How about we name them after the reindeer in the Christmas song?" she asked thoughtfully. "I know it's not very original, but they are Christmas puppies."

"Hmm, I like that idea. Calling out reindeer names over the next couple of weeks will be fun. But what happens after Christmas? Do you think the names will still work?"

"Lots of people name their dog's comet. Dasher and dancer sound like good names, too."

"We should get a sharpie and write their new names on their collars. That way, we won't forget which one is which."

"Sounds good. I'll go grab one from my room," she replied as she stood up.

After a quick trip up and then down the stairs, she was back with a marker. "Okay, she said, picking up the nearest pup. Which one is this little guy going to be?"

"Definitely dancer," he replied, laughing as the little guy danced around in her lap.

Grace dutifully wrote the name on the top of the collar. They went through each dog until they had named them all, leaving out Donner and Blitzen. "Now we need a name for Mama," said Grace, looking over at the dog, still fast asleep on Hunter's leg.

"Should we keep with our Christmas theme and name her Mary?" asked Hunter with a grin.

"I don't know. Some people may get offended by that. How about—"

"Ruby," Granny called out from the doorway to her room. "When I was little, I used to beg my parents for a dog. They always said no, so I would pretend I had one, anyway. I always called her Ruby."

Grace looked up at Granny with a smile. "I love it!"

"I love it too," replied Hunter. "I think it suits her."

"It's even keeping with the Christmas theme since red is one of the most famous Christmas colors!" exclaimed Grace.

"I'm glad you both like it. I would like to keep her if you don't mind?" Granny asked Grace.

"I wouldn't mind at all. I had hoped you'd agree to keep at least Ruby. Finding a home for her will be more challenging than it will for the puppies. Plus, she's so sweet, I fear I'm already attached."

Granny nodded in agreement. "Glad that's settled. Are you two kids ready for lunch? This old bird is starving!"

"Granny!" Grace admonished playfully. "You shouldn't say things like that. You're only as old as you feel."

"Just wait till you're my age. When you have more fake body parts than real, the whole 'age is just a number thing' goes out the window." replied Granny as she slowly walked behind her walker to the dining room.

"We could just call you robogran," Grace teased. "You know, like robocop, only better."

Hunter tried to stifle his laugh but failed. Once he started, it wasn't long before they joined him; the thought of Granny as a butt-kicking robot warrior was too funny not to laugh at.

Finally, they reached the table, collapsing into a chair. "This has been a lot of fun. I'm glad you decided to do this, Grace," said Granny, smiling at the two of them.

"I'm glad I did, too, Granny." Grace smiled back, happier than she had been in as long as she could remember. Granny was doing better. She was getting out of bed at least once a day, talking and laughing, and even planning to keep a dog. Grace was so close to getting her miracle she could feel it.

-Days till Christmas-

Ten

The day she had been waiting for, had worked so hard for, had finally come. Today was the day the guests arrived, and Grace couldn't wait to meet the people she had spent so much time thinking about and putting faces to their names. It was going to be an exciting day.

Due to the special occasion, she took extra time getting ready to give the appearance of a welcoming yet professional woman. The guests should feel at home spending the holidays as one big, happy family, yet she also wanted them to feel they were getting what they paid for. It was a difficult balance to achieve, especially for someone without a clue what she was doing.

Finally happy with her appearance, she went downstairs to the living room. Breakfast had been served hours ago, bedrooms had been given a final inspection, and the bathrooms were sparkling clean. All that was left to do was wait for the guests. She still had to entertain the others, but the puppies had been doing an excellent job of that.

Upon entering the room, she found Molly sitting quietly in the corner, surrounded by sleeping puppies. She was staring out the window and appeared to be lost in thought. Unsure of whether to disturb her, Grace contemplated quietly backing out of the room. Before she could do so, Ruby spotted her and noisily jumped up from her bed to run across the room for some pets.

The commotion brought Molly back to earth. "Hey, Grace, you look nice. Ready for the new guests?"

"I can't wait!" Grace exclaimed. "Where's everyone else?"

"Grant and Hunter went out," Molly explained. "They said they had a few things to take care of, and Gladys and Granny are in Granny's room. They were playing rummy last time I checked on them."

Grace nodded at the explanation. "And how about you? You doing okay?"

"Yeah, I'm fine. Just thinking about the future," she replied. Her smile did not quite reach her eyes.

"Are things still going well with Grant?"

"Yeah," Molly sighed. "They've been going great. We've spent more time together in the last couple of days than in the last few months. It's been wonderful."

"Then what's the problem?"

"What happens when we go back home? Will everything go back to the way it was? I don't think I'll be able to handle the heartbreak if it does."

Before Grace could respond, the doorbell rang. She looked at Molly apologetically. "I'm sorry, but I think that might be Carl."

Molly shook her head. "It's fine. Go greet our new guest. I'll wait for you to come back."

Grace got up to head back down the hallway. When she opened the front door, a tall man with white hair and the bluest eyes she had ever seen greeted her.

"Hello there, you must be Grace."

"And you must be Carl," she replied, smiling warmly. "It's so nice to meet you. Please, come in."

She grabbed one of the bags he had sitting on the porch and led him inside. "How about I show you to your room, and then I'll give you a house tour? Unless, of course, you'd rather rest first?"

"A tour sounds lovely. I've been sitting in the car for hours and would love to stretch my legs."

"Wonderful. This here is the main staircase," she said as she led him up the stairs. "There's another one at the back of the house, but we keep it closed unless there's an emergency."

"Oh, why's that?"

"We call the other stairs the 'death stairs'. They were built for the servants and are extremely steep and narrow. Using that staircase is like playing Russian roulette. You just never know when your time is up."

Carl laughed. "You paint quite the gruesome picture of something that should be fairly innocuous!"

"Just wait till you see the stairs. If you run into any ghosts at night, you'll know what happened to them!"

"That sounds exciting. Are you telling me this is a haunted house?"

Grace shrugged. "Not to my knowledge; I was teasing about the ghosts. Not the stairs, though; they really are dangerous. Here is your room," she said, opening the door to the room closest to her own.

The room was a good size. It had gray walls, hardwood floors with a sizeable gray and white-colored rug, and a full-size bed with an antique headboard. Like the rest of the rooms, it also had a working fireplace with a chair and table in front of it. One of the trees Hunter and Grace had purchased from the store last week stood bare in the corner, awaiting Carl's personal touch.

"It's a beautiful room, Grace. I can already tell I'm going to love it here."

Grace smiled at the kind words. They were just what she wanted to hear. "I'm so glad to hear you say that. A gift basket on the dresser contains coffee, tea, and other goodies from local businesses. All meals are provided, and we have an assortment of beverages and snacks in the kitchen downstairs; you are welcome to help yourself whenever you wish."

Carl placed his luggage on the bed. "That sounds wonderful. I'm ready to tour the rest of the house when you are."

"Yes sir, right this way." Grace led him back into the hall, showing him the three bathrooms and pointing out the rooms everyone else would stay in. After a quick peek at the death stairs, where he agreed they did, in fact, seem rather dangerous, they made their way downstairs.

After passing a small half-bath, they found themselves in the kitchen/dining room combo. She showed him where the food and drinks were kept and then went to the living room. His eyes lit up when he saw the puppies and an expression of pure joy came over his face. "May I pet them?" he asked hopefully.

"Of course! They love attention, so please feel free to spend as much time with them as you'd like."

Carl bent down to pet Ruby first, allowing her to sniff his hands and deem him worthy before he went near her babies. Once he passed the test, he sat down and barked out a laugh as six curious pups made their way over to him. "I see you've given them reindeer names," he said, looking at the writing on their collars.

"We thought it seemed appropriate."

As if noticing Molly for the first time, Carl reached out a hand for her to shake. "Well, hello there, young lady. I'm sorry I didn't see you over there."

Molly smiled as she took his hand. "Nice to meet you," she replied with a chuckle. "It's hard to stand out in a sea of such cuteness."

"Are you one of the guests?" Carl asked.

"Yes, I am. I'm Molly, by the way. My husband, Grant, and another of our guests, Hunter, are also here, but they're out now."

"Ah, some last-minute shopping, perhaps?" he asked with a twinkle in his eye.

Before she could respond, the door to the Granny's room opened, and Granny and Gladys shuffled out behind their walkers. "Oh, I see one of the guests has arrived," said Granny.

Carl got to his feet and helped Grace and Molly move the puppies back into their pen so Granny and Gladys could walk through. Once the path was clear, they slowly moved toward the dining room, where they took their seats. Grace ran to the front door to collect their lunch and then returned to pass out the containers and fill everyone's drink orders. While she took care of that, Molly made the introductions. With that done, everyone dug into their soup and sandwiches.

"I'm very sorry for the loss of your partner," Granny said to Carl between bites. "I hope we can provide at least some comfort during this difficult time."

Carl nodded his head. "Thank you. I really appreciate the sentiment. Christmas was one of our favorite holidays...I just couldn't bear the thought of spending it alone."

"I can certainly understand that. The holidays are the worst for grieving people. I at least had my son when my husband died. He was young, but it forced me to keep going."

"That's what I'm trying to do," Carl replied sadly. "To keep going."

"We're happy to help you do that in any way we can," Gladys replied. "Not to be nosy, but you don't have any kids? Or family?"

"Gladys!" Granny smacked her friend on the arm. "You shouldn't ask such intrusive questions."

Grace tried to hide her smile. It was only a few days ago that Granny was grilling Hunter and Molly with the same questions.

"What?" shrugged Gladys. "At our age, we don't have time to beat around the bush."

Carl chuckled. "It's okay, ladies; I don't mind answering your questions. It would be nice to know a thing or two about the people we're sharing a home with for the next two weeks."

He wiped his face with his napkin and took a long drink of tea. "As to your questions, no, we never had kids, and yes, I technically do have family, but we've been estranged for so long they might as well be dead."

Grace gasped at the sharpness of his words. Despite how nonchalantly he had spoken, there was still a lot of pain in both his words and his eyes. "What happened?" she asked softly.

"Simply put, I couldn't be the person they wanted me to be. My parents had my whole life planned out: what college I would attend, the degree I would major in, and the company I would work for. They had a house picked out, a car, and even my wife. They were convinced they knew exactly what I needed to do and told me that if I listened, I would have a life of happiness." Carl sighed at the memories.

He shook his head sadly, a hint of tears in his eyes. "For a long time, I believed them and did exactly as I was told, but I was miserable. I kept thinking I was the problem and wasn't trying hard enough. Or thankful enough. That I was selfish and entitled. So many people would kill to have my life. To have the opportunities that I had been given. And here, I hated every second of it. Then I met my partner," he said with a smile.

"My partner was a breath of fresh air. It didn't take long for me to realize that I wasn't the problem. The real problem was that I was living the life they wanted, not the life that I wanted. I knew things had to change, but when I told my parents, instead of being understanding and supportive, they were outraged and accused me of being ungrateful and betraying them. They gave me a choice: either I cut all contact with my partner and follow their plan, or I was cut off and could never come home again."

The room was silent, all eyes on Carl. Grace's mouth opened and closed as she tried to process what she'd heard. She had never heard something so horrible. How could a parent treat their own child that way? Granny would never do something like that to her. It was unthinkable. "I'm so sorry," she finally whispered.

Carl smiled and patted her hand. "Thank you, but it was a long time ago. My parents have since passed, so it's been over and done with for years."

"You were never able to reconcile before they passed?" asked Molly.

"I tried a couple of times, but they stood firm in their decision. My siblings, afraid of getting cut off themselves, also cut ties with me. Don't feel too sorry for me, though. I lived a wonderful life, and I don't have a single regret."

The doorbell rang, and Grace excused herself, sorry she would miss the rest of the story. Luckily, it had seemed close to completion, but it felt like leaving the theater when there were still five minutes left in the movie.

Opening the door, she was greeted by a sea of smiling faces. Both of the families had arrived. "Hi everyone, welcome to Winterwood! I'm so excited to meet all of you!" exclaimed Grace.

They all said hello back, well, at least most of them. The teenage boys had their faces buried in their phones, earbuds visible in their ears, likely playing some kind of mobile game. Their parents stepped forward, dragging them along as they walked. "Janet and Greg," the mom said. "And these are our sons, Michael and Mark."

"Pleasure to meet you," Grace smiled. "Your room is up the stairs, first door on the left. If you want to head up, I'll meet you there in a couple of minutes,"

They grabbed their luggage and walked inside, Janet nagging the boys to get off their phones.

"You must be Ryan and Chloe," said Grace to the remaining couple. "And this must be Emma and Theo. I have a surprise I think the two of you will love." The kids looked up at her excitedly. "Let's get you inside so I can give you all a tour of the house."

They picked up their bags and followed her inside when, suddenly, Ryan stopped. "I forgot my laptop in the car. You go on without me. I'll catch up to you in a minute."

"What do you mean you forgot your laptop?" Chloe asked, a weary look in her eyes. "We agreed that this would be an electronics-free vacation. You promised, Ryan."

"Look, babe, you know I can't do that. I'll do my best to spend as much time with the family as possible, but I still have to work."

Chloe shook her head angrily. "This is ridiculous."

"It isn't fair for you to be mad at me. The only reason we can afford little vacations like this in the first place is because of my job. Stop acting like this, or you'll ruin it for everyone."

Grace watched Ryan stomp off toward the car. A quick glance at Chloe showed her, wiping tears from her eyes. This was not a good start to her carefully planned, family-themed, Old-Fashioned Christmas Experience. Grace wasn't the only one who needed a Christmas miracle.

-Days till Christmas-

Nine

"Okay, listen up everybody, it's time to head over to the tree farm," Grace announced to the crowd gathered around the dining room table. "Is everyone ready to go?"

The heads that weren't buried in their phones all nodded enthusiastically.

"Awesome! To make this as painless as possible, we will take three cars. The two families will take their vehicles, and the rest of us will squeeze into Hunter's truck. A local named Junior has agreed to meet us there to help transport the tree back home. Questions?"

Grace looked around the room and saw Theo raise his hand. "Yes, Theo?"

"How big of a tree can we get?"

"We should be safe with a tree eight feet tall or less. Gotta leave room for the angel!"

"Will it be a real tree?" asked Emma.

"Yes, sweetheart, it will be a real tree," said Grace, smiling warmly at the adorable little girl. "And I believe they will have hot cocoa and cookies for us when we get there."

"What about the puppies? Can they come too?" asked Theo, his arms wrapped protectively around one of the little guys.

"I'm afraid not. They're too little to leave their mama right now, but they will be waiting for us when we get back. Then, you can put the ornaments you made for them on the tree. Won't that be fun?"

Both kids nodded their heads, a serious expression on their faces. Grace had to try pretty hard not to laugh. They had all had a wonderful time the night before making personalized ornaments for the Christmas tree. Even the older boys had gotten into it. The kids had been so thrilled when they met the puppies; they had insisted on making ornaments for them, too.

Grace had taken lots of pictures but was thrilled she would have a physical reminder of the memories she was making. These ornaments will grace her Christmas tree for years to come.

"If there are no more questions, we should get going." Grace grabbed her coat, hat, and gloves and led the way to the front door, eleven people following behind.

Granny and Gladys had decided to sit this one out. The cold and all the walking were too much for them. Grace had been disappointed at first, but they had promised to help with the decorating afterward, so she let it go. Besides, it really would have been too much. She wanted Granny to get better, not catch pneumonia.

Grace, Molly, and Grant piled into the backseat of Hunter's truck. Carl sat in the front passenger seat while

Hunter drove. It was crowded but cozy. Almost all of them were strangers, yet it felt like they were old friends, laughing and joking as they passed the time.

Twenty minutes later, they arrived at Lyle's Tree Farm. Grace searched the parking lot and was relieved when she saw Junior's old, beat-up Chevy parked by the exit. Perfect, if everyone can quickly agree on a tree, they should be able to make it back home with plenty of time to decorate and hold the snowman contest.

They huddled together for a moment while they discussed the plan. "Do you guys want to split into groups of two or stay together in a group of one?" asked Grace.

"I think it might be easier to split up," replied Carl. "Those aisles don't look very big."

"If no one minds, those of us with kids can be in one group, and the ones without can be in the other," suggested Janet.

Grace nodded. "That should work. Each group can pick a tree, then we'll vote to see which one we get. That sound good?"

Everyone nodded, so they split into their prospective groups. Grace smiled as the family group headed straight for the restrooms. "Alright, guys," said Grace, addressing her group. "If my memory is correct, the trees are in sections based on height and type. So all we need to do is follow the signs, and they should lead us to the type of tree we're looking for."

"Do you really want to get a tree that's eight feet tall?" asked Hunter. "That's a lot of tree to wrangle."

"We don't have to get a tree that big; that's just the biggest that will fit. It would fill the space up nicely, though. So it might be worth it," Grace shrugged.

"Let's just see what they have," said Molly. "We can start with the six-foot trees and work our way up."

They agreed to the plan and set off toward the trees. When they got to the six-footers, they immediately agreed they were too small, the male members of their party towering over them. The seven-footers were better height-wise, but the few left were too skinny. The eight-foot ones held some promise, but none jumped out at them as 'the one.'

Grace was beginning to feel deflated when Emma and Chloe ran over to get their attention. "We found one!" yelled Emma. "Come see, come see."

She grabbed Grace's hand and pulled, leaving Grace no choice but to follow. Laughing at the little girl's enthusiasm, she called out to the others.

When they reached the family group, Grace saw they were standing before a nine-foot Frasier fir tree. It was a monster of a tree, but it was indeed perfect. She loved it and could tell by the looks on everyone else's faces they loved it, too.

"Can we make it work?" Hunter whispered in her ear.

She turned to look up at him. "I don't know. The ceilings are ten feet high. That only leaves one foot for the angel and the stand. What do you think?"

"It'll be tight, but we might be able to trim it down enough to make it fit," he reasoned. "It's a lot of tree and will take a lot of help to manhandle it into place."

"I think it will be worth it," Grace assured him.

Hunter nodded. "Then let's do it."

Grace grinned, then turned back to face the group. "Does everyone agree this is the one?"

They cheered in response. "Awesome! I'll go get Lyle and Junior so we can get to work on getting this bad boy home."

***

It took two hours to cut the tree down, load it in the back of Junior's truck, and get it home and in place in the living room. Then, another two hours to string the lights, hang the ornaments, and wrap the garland. Adding in the time it took for their lunch break, it was now late afternoon.

Everyone bundled up and headed outside for the snowman-building competition. Granny and Gladys had helped decorate the tree but had again opted out of the more physical activity. It had been more difficult for Grace to hide her disappointment this time, as the snowman competition had been one of Granny's favorite memories to share.

Her practical side understood that Granny, who needed a walker to get around, was incapable of doing the task. Her emotional side was worried that Granny was missing out on all the important activities. Could her plan still work if Granny couldn't relive the memories of her youth?

As if sensing her distress, Hunter walked over to talk. "Don't worry about Granny. She's doing fine."

"You really think so? I'm doing all this for her, and she keeps missing out on all the important activities."

"Since I've been here, she's come out of her room daily for lunch and dinner. She's had multiple conversations with the guests and participated last night with the decorations and this afternoon."

"I know it's just..."

"Grace, she's an eighty-five-year-old woman with health problems. While I believe she still has a lot of life left in her, we can't forget she has limitations. Try to focus on the positive and let go of the rest, okay?"

When she nodded, he continued. "Good, now it looks like we're partners. What do you say we show these guys how to make a proper snowman?"

Grace looked around and saw that everyone else had partnered off. Molly and Grant, Janet and Greg, Ryan and Theo, and Chloe and Emma worked in pairs. Carl, Mark, and Michael were also working together, although they had more fun throwing snowballs at each other than building a snowman. Everyone was smiling and having a good time. Grace could see that even Granny and Gladys appeared to be smiling as they watched through the windows of the french doors.

"Let's do this," Grace replied with a laugh.

Thirty minutes later, they had five snowmen and two forts ready for judging. Mayor Allen showed up, in his official capacity, to judge the competition. After greeting all the guests, he made a show of inspecting each snowman.

"Attention, I have made my decision," he announced. "The snowman with the pretty pink scarf and matching hat is the winner."

Realizing it was her snowman, Emma squealed in delight. Mayor Allen gave her an official handshake, and Grace took their picture, promising to send each a copy. The mayor even gave an honorable mention to the boys for their creativity in building the forts.

"I would like to give a very warm thank you to Mayor Allen for coming out tonight," said Grace. "And I would like to invite all of you to go inside, where I have hot cocoa and mulled cider ready to help warm you up."

"Is it time for the angel?" asked Emma.

"Yes, it is," Grace smiled. "Are you ready?"

Emma nodded as she smiled shyly. They walked inside, and Grace got busy handing out drinks. That done, she pulled the angel out of its box.

"This is really fragile, so we have to be careful, okay," she said to Emma.

"I promise," she whispered, clearly taking this very seriously.

"We're going to need someone to help you. Ryan?" Grace asked, looking around for Emma's dad.

When she couldn't find him, Chloe appeared at her side, seething with anger. "He went upstairs to make a call. Claimed it couldn't wait." she spat.

"Um, okay, well," Grace looked around the room for another volunteer, grateful when Carl stepped forward.

"I don't mind helping out if that's okay with you?" Carl asked Chloe.

Chloe nodded in agreement. Carl had Emma climb the ladder as he followed closely behind. When they reached the top, Hunter handed Carl the angel, who gave it to Emma. Carl held her steady as she leaned over to place the angel on the tree.

Once in place, they carefully climbed back down, and everyone stood back to admire their handiwork.

"It's beautiful," said Grace to no one in particular.

The rest of the crowd nodded in agreement. Grace looked at Granny and saw that she had tears in her eyes. Walking over to her, she sat beside her on the couch and put her arms around her. "Why are you crying?" she asked.

"It's a beautiful moment," Granny replied, patting Grace on the back. "I'm going to remember this for the rest of my life. Thank you, Grace."

"I'm going to remember it, too, and if we ever come close to forgetting, I took enough pictures to last a lifetime!"

Granny laughed. "That sounds wonderful, dear. I hope you're happy. After all your hard work, you deserve it."

Grace laid her head on Granny's shoulder. "I am happy. All I wanted was a special Christmas with you."

They sat quietly as they watched the others talk and laugh. It was a happy scene, full of happy people. Day two had been a success. Nine more to go until the big day.

-Days till Christmas-

Eight

The day of the Christmas festival had finally arrived. It officially started at ten, but Grace and the other committee members had been running around since seven that morning, seeing to last-minute details. Grace had never felt so tired and yet so excited before in her life. Once everything was as good as it would get, they stood back to wait for what they hoped would be crowds of people to show up.

It was a beautiful day for a winter festival. The meteorologist predicted the temperature to be around thirty degrees, but the sky was clear, and the sun was shining. Fire pits were scattered throughout the park for added warmth, and plenty of stands provided hot cocoa and cider. In addition, there were vendors selling food, games for the children to play, local artisans selling their wares, and mini carnival rides.

Later that afternoon, there will be a chili cook-off and a pie-baking competition, and, of course, no festival would be complete without an appearance from Santa. When you factored in the parade, the tree lighting ceremony, and the concert later that night, they had a full day ahead of them.

A quarter after ten, Grace saw the group from her make-shift inn arrive. She lived close enough to the park for everyone to walk; from what she could tell, that's precisely what they did. However, it looked like a couple of people were missing.

Spotting Molly, Grace hurried over to see if she knew what was going on. "Hey, Molly, where are the guys?" she asked, referring to Hunter, Grant, and Ryan.

"I believe Ryan is back at the house working. He's supposed to be joining his family around lunchtime. As for Hunter and Grant, I have no idea. I haven't seen either of them all morning. When I tried to call Grant, it went straight to voice mail."

"That's strange. I wonder what they're up to?"

"I don't know," Molly shook her head. "I wonder..." she trailed off without finishing her thought.

"Wonder what?" asked Grace.

"I don't know, it's just that Grant's been acting strange these past few days, almost secretive. It sounds ridiculous, but I've wondered if he's having an affair."

Grace gasped in shock. "Surely not. He quit his job and came all the way down here to win you back. I can't believe he would do that if he had another woman on the side."

"Grant and I grew apart a long time ago. Is it really so far out of the realm of possibility that he could have found someone else?"

"If that were true, why not let you go? Why go to all this trouble?"

Molly thought about it for a moment. "I guess you're right, but if another woman isn't the cause of his behavior, what is?"

"Maybe he's working on a special Christmas present? It is that time of year, and I doubt he had time to get you something before he came here."

Molly nodded, looking somewhat appeased. "That would make sense. I should trust him until he gives me a reason not to."

"Exactly," responded Grace, laying her hand on Molly's arm. "How about you check out the booths we have set up around the park? You might find a present for Grant. You don't want to be empty-handed on Christmas morning, especially if he shows up with a fistful of diamonds!"

They shared a laugh, and then Molly continued on her way. A few minutes later, Grace came upon Janet and Greg. "Good morning, you two! Enjoying the festival so far?"

Janet groaned and rolled her eyes. "We would be if it wasn't for our sons refusing to get off their stupid phones."

"We threatened to take them away," explained Greg. "But they would only mope around, and we still wouldn't have any fun."

Grace thought about it for a minute. Spotting a couple of boys from the high school, she devised a plan. "Give me a couple of minutes, and I'll see if there's something I can do to help you."

She took off in the direction she had just seen the boys go and finally caught up with them at one of the fire pits. "Hey guys," she said, a little out of breath from running after them. "I have a favor to ask."

"Sure. What's up?" asked Jason, the boy from the first meeting and, from what Grace could tell, the football team's quarterback.

"You see those two boys over there?" she said, pointing at Mark and Michael. "Their parents are having a hard time getting them off their phones. They're at that age where they really want to be cool, so—"

"Say no more," Jason interrupted, a grin on his face. "We know exactly what to do, don't we guys?"

Grace watched them walk over to Mark and Michael, hopeful they understood what she was asking. From a distance, she saw Mark and Michael were in awe of Jason. She breathed a sigh of relief when Jason and the others appeared to be organizing an impromptu football game. Soon, a large group of kids and parents gathered at the far edge of the park. She smiled when she saw Greg, Janet, and the boys among them. They were going to make some memories after all.

Several hours passed, with Grace alternating between checking on her guests and checking on all the vendors. She put out fires where needed, ran errands, and covered for those needing bathroom breaks. When she finally had a moment to catch her breath, she stumbled upon Ryan and Chloe in the midst of an argument.

"All you ever do is work, work, work," Chloe shouted. "You promised things would be different. That you would actually be a part of this family. So far, all you've done is work."

"Would you please keep your voice down," Ryan said quietly as he looked around to see if anyone was listening. "I never said I wouldn't work. You booked an eleven-day trip. How could I possibly go that long without working?"

"I don't know, Ryan. You should take one of those things I keep hearing about. What are they called? Oh yeah, a vacation. That's what normal people do."

Ryan sighed, running his hand through his hair in frustration. "You know I can't do that, especially not at the last minute. Jeez, Chloe, I'm doing the best I can."

"Yeah, well, your best isn't good enough. I'm done, Ryan; I want a divorce." Chloe turned on her heel and stomped away. Even from a distance, Grace could see that she was crying.

Walking up behind him, she put her hand on his shoulder. "You okay?" Grace asked sympathetically.

Ryan shook his head. "No, I'm not. I'm guessing you heard?"

"I wasn't trying to eavesdrop, but yes, I heard."

"I don't know what to do. I don't want a divorce, but nothing seems to ever be good enough for her."

"It's none of my business, and I am definitely not a marriage expert, but I don't think Chloe wants a divorce, either. What she really wants is more time with you," Grace replied softly.

"How do I give her that?" Ryan asked with a sigh. "Chloe and I had a plan. She would stay home with the kids while they were young and return to work when they reached school age. We had enough money put aside to see us through, but..."

"But what?"

"But we didn't realize how difficult and expensive it would be. Once the kids reached school age, someone still had to be available to get them to school and pick them up afterward. Then there was summer vacation, teacher in-service days, holidays, early release days," Ryan said, ticking each one off his fingers. "Daycare programs only filled in for some of those, cost an arm and a leg, and don't cover sick days. By the time we added up the cost of childcare and compared it to the income Chloe would bring in, we barely broke even."

Ryan sighed again, pacing back and forth in front of her. "We decided Chloe would continue to be a stay-at-home mom, but that meant I would need to find a way to bring in more money. Which, of course, led to me having to work more. I don't want to work all these hours, but I have no choice. And now she's mad at me on top of it. I can't win!"

Grace took a step back, unsure of what to say. This was way above her pay grade, and she wanted to refrain from saying or doing something to make things worse. After a few minutes of silence, she thought of something to ask. "Have you told Chloe everything you just told me?"

Ryan stopped pacing and turned to look at her. "Not really. I figured she knew. How could she not?"

"Sometimes things that seem obvious to us are not obvious to others, especially when emotions are involved. Where are the kids?"

"They're with Carl. He took them to get their faces painted."

"How about this? I'll help Carl entertain the kids, and you can talk to Chloe. Tell her everything you told me."

"I don't know, she's really upset. Maybe I should wait until she's had time to calm down."

"Trust me, that's the last thing you want to do. If you don't go after her now, she will see this as a sign that you don't care about her. It will only cement her belief that you should divorce."

"Okay, you're right. I'll go," he said, walking in the direction Chloe went. "Thanks, Grace," he called over his shoulder.

Grace nodded and searched for Carl and the kids, hopeful she'd said the right thing. She wanted them to work things out, so she silently prayed, asking for another miracle. Spotting Carl, Grace hurried over to him and the kids. "Looks like we're going to need to babysit a little longer," she said with a smile.

Carl nodded, understanding in his eyes. "How about we play some more games?" he asked the kids. "I think I saw a couple with prizes you could win."

Excited at the thought of winning a prize, the kids eagerly agreed. Carl and Grace spent the next couple of hours alternating between games, snacks, and even a trip to see Santa. By the time the parade came around, they weren't sure who was more tired, them or the kids. It had been a lot of fun, and Grace had taken a ton of pictures, but they were relieved when they saw Ryan and Chloe heading in their direction.

As Carl and Grace handed off the sleepy kids, Grace was delighted to see both Ryan and Chloe had huge smiles on their faces. It looked like they had worked things out. As they lined up to catch the end of the parade, Grace saw Ryan mouth the words' thank you' when Chloe wasn't looking. She nodded in response, glad to see that her assumption had been correct.

Pride filled Grace's heart when the floats passed by. The kids at the schools had done a fantastic job. Given their short time to pull this off, what they'd accomplished was nothing short of amazing. Then, when it was time for

Mayor Allen to flip the switch on the Christmas tree, she oohed and aahed with the rest of them.

Looking around as if for the first time, Grace saw the crowds packing the park. It would be a few days before official numbers came out, but their hard work had paid off. And they still had several more days of activities to go.

Her work for the day finally over; Grace turned to walk home, running into Hunter along the way. "Hey, haven't seen you all day," he said.

"I've been around. Did you have a good time?" she asked.

"Yeah, are you going home?"

Grace nodded. "I don't think I'm going to last much longer."

"You're going to miss the concert."

"True, but I have a feeling I might miss it even if I'm there. I'm so tired, I can barely move my feet!" she laughed.

"Looks like I better walk you home, then. Wouldn't want you to end up face-planting somewhere along the way."

"Thanks, but you should stay. The band is great."

"Nah, I think I'm good for the day," he replied, sliding her arm through his.

They walked in silence; Grace too tired to make small talk. When they reached the house, Hunter helped her up the stairs and to the door of her room. "Next time, I hope we'll be able to spend some time together," he said.

Grace nodded. "I would like that. Next up is the sleigh ride. It will be a lot of fun but a lot more low-key."

"I'm looking forward to it. Good night, Grace," he said, gently squeezing her hand.

"Good night, Hunter."

She entered her room, closed the door, and promptly sprawled on her bed. It had been a long day but a good day. Only eight more to go till Christmas.

-Days till Christmas-

Seven

Grace sighed as the computer screen before her flashed twenty-seven possible matches. She had spent the last thirty minutes attempting to find Carl's siblings. An impossible task when you consider she has no idea how many siblings he has, whether they are brothers or sisters, and where they might be located. The only thing she knew for sure was that Carl's last name was Richmond. Not as common as Smith or Jones, but not exactly rare either.

There had to be a way to narrow the list of potential siblings. Maybe she could start a conversation when everyone was at the dining table later and get him to answer some questions without him realizing what she was doing. Other than that, she might have to give up on her plan. That or message twenty-seven people to see if they have an estranged brother named Carl.

Frustrated by her lack of success, she went back downstairs to check on breakfast. She had been up at the usual time of six thirty, had breakfast set out, and had been ready to go by six forty-five. When no one had shown up by seven fifteen, she returned to her room to try her hand at a bit of detective work. After the long day everyone had yesterday, she wasn't surprised to see they were all sleeping in. In fact, she wouldn't have minded being able to do so herself, but so were the woes of an innkeeper, it seemed. Next time, if there was a next time, breakfast would start at seven.

The dining room was still empty, but she found Molly drinking coffee and playing with the puppies in the living room. "Good morning," said Grace cheerfully. "How was the festival? Any luck finding a present for Grant?"

"Not really," said Molly, a strange look on her face. "I looked around, but nothing really stood out to me. At some point, I realized I no longer knew my husband."

"Maybe you need time to get to know each other again. Have you guys ever talked about taking a trip together somewhere?"

"We're already on a trip," Molly replied. "Lately, I've barely seen him, let alone been able to spend any quality time with him. Did you know he didn't even show up at the festival until after three?"

"First of all, this is not the kind of trip I was referring to. I was talking about a romantic trip for two, somewhere private, not a group vacation with a bunch of strangers. Second of all, Grant was out with Hunter yesterday. I'm sure they have a good reason for being gone for so long."

Molly shrugged. "Even still, the whole point of him coming down here was for us to spend time together. I just wish I knew what's going on with him. It would make things so much easier."

"Maybe you should try talking to him. You should have him take you to the Italian restaurant Hunter and I went to. It's private, and the food is delicious. When you're done, you can go look at the lights. It will be romantic," Grace said with a smile.

"Are you saying you went on a romantic date with Hunter? And you didn't tell me?"

"Of course not. It was more of a friend thing when we went, but it would definitely be romantic for people who aren't friends," Grace stammered, a blush creeping up her cheeks.

"You wanted it to be a date, though, didn't you?" Molly asked softly.

"Hunter is only here till the end of the month," replied Grace. "After that, it's back to his life in New York. I'm not interested in being someone's holiday fling."

"Good morning, ladies," said Hunter, yawning as he entered the room. "Am I interrupting?" he asked, looking from one face to the other.

"N-no," Grace replied hurriedly. "I was just telling Molly about Bella's. I thought it would be a nice place for her and Grant to have dinner."

Hunter smiled widely. "That's a great idea. You can go see the lights when you're done with dinner!"

"That's what Grace was saying," said Molly, looking back and forth at them with a curious expression. "I guess that settles it. I'll let Grant know he's taking me there tonight."

"You won't regret it," Hunter said, still smiling. "What's on the agenda for today?" he asked Grace.

Grace looked at her watch. "Bea is going to be here around eleven. The plan is to bake sugar cookies and then decorate them. We also have some gingerbread house-building kits for the more adventurous."

"Hmm, I thought I was told there would be a sleigh ride?" Hunter asked quizzically.

"We planned to do that today, but Junior is busy at the festival, so we've decided to do it tomorrow. Granny will give a history of the town while we're out."

"The sleigh is big enough for all of us to fit at once?" asked Molly.

"Junior's going to break it up into two groups. Granny will go in one, and Gladys will go in the other. Gladys has lived here almost as long as Granny, so she's just as qualified. Although, I have been hearing rumors of some kind of competition, so who knows!"

"This sounds interesting. Those two are quite the hoot when they're together," said Hunter.

"They really are. I have a lot of amusing childhood memories of those two. They worked hard to make up for my growing up without my parents."

Molly smiled. "You're fortunate to have them; I know they feel the same about you."

"Thank you," replied Grace, as she nodded her head. "Now, it's time for you to make plans with Grant while I prepare the kitchen for our next adventure."

Grace marched into the kitchen, expecting them to follow. When they didn't, she turned around to see that they were talking, their heads close together so as not to be overheard. She briefly wondered what they were discussing, then chastised herself for being nosy. It was none of her business, and for the sake of both her heart and sanity, it was time for her to cease blurring the lines between business and personal. These people were paying guests, not friends or family. The sooner she got that through her head, the better it would be.

***

By the time eleven o'clock rolled around, the breakfast dishes had been done, and the dining room had been cleaned, just in time for a new mess to be made. All the guests, including Granny and Gladys, gathered around the dining table, a square of cookie dough rolled out in front of them. Easy-to-reach baking sheets lined the center of the table, awaiting the bells, Christmas trees, and candy canes to be cut and placed upon them.

Grace and Bea passed out an assortment of cookie cutters to each guest and then showed them how to use them. Once that was done, Grace pulled out her camera and took pictures. Everything was going well until Emma screamed. "Stop telling me what to do. I'm not a baby."

"I wouldn't have to tell you what to do if you weren't doing it wrong," Theo yelled back.

"I am not. You're just being bossy," Emma pouted.

"And you're being a big poopy baby," replied Theo, sticking his tongue out at her.

"Hey, you two, knock it off," said Ryan in an attempt to intervene.

Grace looked over at Emma's cookies and saw that she was struggling to get them off the table without smushing them. She motioned to Bea, who hurried over to see if she could help. Recognizing this as an opportunity, Grace decided to ask a question. "Do siblings always fight like this?" she asked, sounding as lighthearted as possible.

A room full of heads all turned toward her and nodded vigorously.

"Especially when they're young," replied Granny.

"Oh, the stories I could tell," Janet chimed in. "I think sisters might just be the worst!" she laughed.

"I would be willing to agree with that," Hunter grinned.

"Oh, I don't know," said Carl. "I had one of each, and as the youngest, my siblings would probably agree that brothers are the worst!"

Perfect! Just what she needed to know. The banter continued for a few minutes, but she tuned it out, a new plan already forming in her mind. Now that she knew who she was looking for, it was time to see if she could figure out where.

Once the room was quiet again, Grace asked another question. "So, I know we have several northerners here with us. How about the rest of you? Is everybody else from around here?"

The two families had come from the state next door and confirmed they had grown up there. She, of course, knew where everyone else had come from, so all that was left was Carl. "I'm from down south originally. From the great state of Louisiana!"

"Wow! That's exciting!" replied Grace, trying to sound cheerful yet nonchalant. Inside, she was doing a happy dance and giving herself a high five. She still didn't have names and had no idea if his siblings still lived in Louisiana or, like their brother, had moved, but it was a hundred times more information than she'd had that morning. Surely, this was enough to at least start her search.

With the cookies in the oven, they decided to work on the gingerbread houses while they waited. The cookies needed to bake and cool before it was time to decorate, and that could take at least an hour. They split into groups, the kids in one group, parents in another, Molly, Grant, and Hunter in one, and Granny, Gladys, and Carl in another.

It didn't take long for it to turn into a competition. By the time everyone was done, there were several categories to judge. Which team finished first, had the tallest house, and did the best decorating. Bea and Grace had the unfortunate job of choosing between them.

Which team was the fastest was easy; the parents finished several minutes before everyone else; it was obviously not their first rodeo. The tallest was also easy. They had to get a ruler, but Hunter, Molly, and Grant were the obvious winners. The third one was the hardest. Neither Grace nor Bea wanted to hurt anyone's feelings, yet they had to choose one. After several minutes of deliberation over how they would break the news, they finally announced the winners: Carl, Granny, and Gladys. Their design was meticulous, and the reason they lost out on who was fastest. They simply spent more time on the details.

The only ones who didn't win were the kids. Grace felt bad but offered them cookies as a consolation prize, which seemed enough to cheer them up. After passing out all the baked and cooled cookies, they set out bowls of colored frosting and a multitude of sprinkles in all shapes, colors, and sizes. Both kids and adults gleefully laughed and chattered as they added pops of color to their otherwise beige cookies.

Grace was on picture duty once more. Fifteen minutes later, the cookies were done, and the ones that hadn't been eaten were put away for later. "I just want to let you know the festival is still going on if any of you want to check it out before it ends at six," Grace reminded everyone.

Ryan and Chloe, having missed most of it the day before, decided to take the kids. To the surprise of both of their parents, Mark and Michael also wanted to go, likely hoping for another football game. Molly and Grant chose to head up to the city for their date a bit early, and Gladys and Granny declared it was time for their daily naps, which left Hunter and Grace.

"What are your plans for the afternoon?" Hunter asked Grace as he helped her clean up the cookie mess.

"It looks like now would be a good time to do some cleaning since everyone is going out."

"No rest for the weary," he said with a smile.

"Doesn't appear to be," she replied with a wry grin. "What about you? Are you going back to the festival?"

"Nah, I thought I might stick around and see if a certain innkeeper needs help?"

"You don't have to do that," she said, shaking her head. "Scrubbing toilets is no one's definition of a vacation."

"It's your holiday too, Grace. You don't have to spend it like Cinderella."

"I think that's exactly what I signed up for when I devised this elaborate plan, and it's okay, I'm happy to do it."

Hunter looked at her like he didn't believe her but held his tongue. Which was just as well; she had zero intention of ever admitting how much she disliked certain aspects of running an inn.

Finished in the kitchen, she headed upstairs, Hunter trailing behind her. She had expected him to go to his room, so she was surprised when he followed her into the bathroom instead. "It'll be faster if I help," he said with a shrug.

She tried to argue, but he reached over and put a finger to her lips. "No arguing. It's my decision to help. For all you know, I like to clean." He gave her a mischievous look, and she couldn't help but laugh.

"Fine, you win! But only because I don't want to do this alone."

"We could always turn this into another competition," he waggled his eyebrows.

"Oh yeah, what would the winner get?"

"Let's see. If I win, I get blueberry waffles with sausage and maple syrup for breakfast every day this week."

"You can already have that, silly. I just need to let Bea know."

He shrugged. "If you win, I will give you a special surprise."

"How do I know I'll like this surprise? It could be something awful, like dirty socks! Not a lot of motivation, if you ask me."

"I said 'special' surprise. Dirty socks are not special," Hunter said with mock indignation. "Besides, I thought you were the kind of girl who liked mysteries. Don't you want to find out what the surprise is?"

"Well, when you put it that way, you're on!"

They got to work, each one picking a bathroom to clean. When finished, she ran down the hall to see if Hunter was done. When she entered the bathroom, he was still scrubbing the toilet. "Looks like I win," she said, grinning from ear to ear.

He surprised her by smiling back. "Looks like you did. Guess I owe you that surprise."

"So what is it?" she asked, a gleam in her eyes. She had spent the last twenty minutes trying to guess what it could be and had come up with everything, from one of his cookies to a trip to Disneyland. The last part was ridiculous but fun to dream about.

"If I told you, it wouldn't be a surprise!"

"Then when do I get it?"

"Soon, I promise."

Grace rolled her eyes. It figures he'd make her wait, but at least the bathrooms were clean. That in itself was a prize. Oh well, she'd just have to be patient. Plenty of time to dream about that trip to Disney.

-Days till Christmas-

Six

"Granny, are you sure you're feeling up to this?" asked Grace as she helped Granny bundle up in her winter coat. "It's freezing out there."

"I'll be fine, dear. We'll have plenty of blankets and hot cocoa to keep us warm," she replied, excitement in her clear green eyes. "I've been looking forward to this since you told me about it."

Granny's assurances did little to ease Grace's over-protective fears, but she kept her mouth shut and continued working on getting her ready. Today was the day for the sleigh ride; well, not really a sleigh ride, so much as a horse-drawn carriage ride, but it was close enough. They'd decorated the horses and carriages to resemble something out of a Dickens Christmas scene, which helped set the mood for the old-fashioned Christmas experience they were trying to provide.

Everyone had been looking forward to it, including Grace. Junior and his friend had old-fashioned, open-air, horse-drawn carriages; they usually only pulled them out for parades or the local antique fair held once a year. They both graciously agreed to give rides during the festival, and now they would provide Grace's guests a personalized tour of the town. Granny and Gladys would narrate the tours, giving everyone a small history lesson as they went along.

After Granny was ready to go, Grace checked on the rest of the guests. From what she could see, they were busy donning hats, gloves, and scarves; Ryan and Chloe ensuring Emma and Theo were dressed warmly enough. That done, she moved on to the kitchen to check on the thermoses of hot cocoa. She was providing two per carriage, along with a stack of paper cups and a tin of cookies. Add the cozy blankets; they will have everything they need for the perfect afternoon outing.

The doorbell rang, and Grace ran to answer it, finding Junior on the other side of the door.

"Hey, Grace, can we talk for a minute?" asked Junior, looking everywhere but at her.

"Um, sure," Grace replied, stepping onto the porch and closing the door behind her. She really hoped he wasn't about to back out on them. If he did, she would have fourteen disappointed people with no backup plan to distract them.

"Can you tell me again how many people we're supposed to be taking out this afternoon?"

"Fifteen, why?"

"I was afraid that's what you were going to say. Each carriage can only fit eight, two in the front and six in the back. That's sixteen total if you count both carriages."

Grace shook her head. "Okay, I don't see where the problem is."

"If you count Ray and me, that makes seventeen," Junior said apologetically.

Grace did the math a few times, hoping she would discover he was wrong. When she didn't, her heart sank. When she had initially made the plans, she hadn't anticipated Grant showing up. In fact, she hadn't even known he existed. And when they did find out, an extra person hadn't seemed like such a big deal until now.

"Okay, it's not a problem," Grace replied. "I'll go get everyone if you're ready?"

Junior nodded his head, so Grace put on her biggest smile and went back inside. "Can I have everyone's attention?" she called out loudly enough to be heard over the chattering.

Once everyone quieted down, Grace gave out the instructions. "Junior and Ray are ready and waiting for you outside," she began, pausing while everyone cheered. "We will split into two groups: Gladys, Janet, Greg, Michael, Mark, Grant, and Molly will go with Ray. Everyone else will go with Junior. Anyone who needs one last bathroom break, please do so now. The rest of you, let's head outside."

Grace grabbed the baskets of cocoa and cookies and followed everyone outside. She went to the side of each carriage, handing the basket to the person closest to the door. Once done, the horses took off, leaving Grace behind. Putting on a brave face, she smiled and waved to the people who noticed, then went inside once they were out of sight.

Swiping tears from the corner of her eyes, she went to the living room to see the puppies. It was tough to stay sad when seven happy dogs were waiting to greet her. Taking a seat on the floor, she hugged each of them, then took turns throwing the toys they brought her to play fetch with, surprised when one was a gnome chew toy. She shook her head and laughed. These things really were turning up everywhere.

An hour later, the group returned, red-cheeked and smiling from ear to ear. Even the kids looked cheerful, talking and laughing about things they'd learned. Grace was a little jealous and disappointed to have been unable to join them, but she was happy that everyone had a good time.

Out of the corner of her eye, she saw Hunter approach.

"You didn't come with us," he stated quietly.

She tried to smile. "There was a lot to do around here. Seemed like a good time to take care of things since everyone was busy and out of the house."

"Hmm," he said, a curious expression on his face. "It's time for your special surprise. I'm going to need you to put your coat back on and come outside with me," he took her hand and pulled her toward the door.

Grace tried to protest. It was almost dinnertime, and she had a hungry group to feed, but he waved her off, explaining that Molly had things under control. With a shrug of her shoulders, she put on her 'winter armor,' as they liked to call it, and followed him outside. Junior was still there, Granny seated on the bench next to him. "What's going on?" asked Grace.

"It's time for you to enjoy one of these activities for once," Hunter responded, helping her into the carriage. "You've been doing so much for everyone else; I thought it was time someone did something for you."

Grace looked at him, her eyes wide. "You don't have to—"

"None of that," he interrupted, covering her with a blanket. "Granny has a fascinating story to tell, and of all the people to hear it, you're the most important one. It's your family, too, after all."

"I don't know what to say," Grace said, wiping tears from her eyes for the second time that afternoon.

"You don't need to say anything. Just listen."

Hunter put his arm around her shoulders, huddling together to stay warm. Granny turned in the front seat to talk as Junior started down the street. One block later, Granny began to speak.

"The house on the right was once a three-story doctor's office and hospital. In the forties, it was bought by a family, and they remodeled it, removing the third story. No one knew why, but the story at the time was that it was haunted by the patients that died up there," Granny said in a spooky voice.

Grace smiled. She had lived down the street from that house for decades and had never known it to be anything other than someone's home.

Granny continued. "The funeral home up here on the left has been there for well over a hundred years. They used to cast the gravestones there, too. It's been a family business for as long as I can remember. They are the ones who buried your ancestors," Granny said, looking pointedly at Grace.

They passed a couple of churches, though they were newer buildings, and then they passed the town hall. "The building on the left was once a manufacturing plant, oh, about a hundred years ago or so. They employed hundreds of locals. And the Masonic Lodge once stood where the library is now. It burned down many decades ago, one of four fires they withstood throughout their history."

Grace was surprised to hear that. The current Masonic lodge was on the outskirts of town. She wasn't sure if they were still active, although they must be to some degree since the building still belonged to them.

"Now we get to the good part," Granny said as they stopped at the corner of Main Street. It was late enough in the afternoon that the Christmas lights were on all over town. Grace was still amazed at the transformation Main Street had undergone. Here, in the carriage, it felt magical.

"At one point, we had two major railroads in town. Passenger trains came through here at least twice daily, once in the morning, where it would stop for breakfast, and once in the evening, where it stopped for dinner. They would eat at McLain's Restaurant. Cattle ranchers from one end of the state to the other would drive their cattle here to load them onto the cattle cars. The ranchers would stay in that old hotel over there in the corner," Granny said, pointing to a large, three-story, red-brick building.

"It was a lot grander at that time. At one point, it even had a dining room and an ice cream parlor."

Grace tried to imagine it as Granny described; a difficult task due to the current run-down state of the building. Most of the windows were boarded up, and there were rumors of rotting floors and mold having overtaken a large part of the hotel. A few people had owned it over the years, but no one had done much with it. At this point, it probably needed more work than was practical, which was a shame considering its history.

"Across from the hotel, where the bar currently sits, used to be the train station. I'm sure it's hard to imagine, but we also had a bus line that ran in the forties and fifties. There are rumors that the stagecoach had a stop here just outside of town to the west."

Junior turned left onto Main Street and continued down the road. "On the left was a livery, a drugstore containing a soda shop, a bicycle and shoe repair store, and a theatre showing black and white silent movies. On the right was a produce store, a bakery, a furniture store, and a large department store. We also had barber shops, where men could take baths, jewelry stores, lawyers, butchers, two newspapers, a laundry house, and two lumber yards."

Granny paused to take a breath while Hunter got out the hot chocolate and handed everyone a drink. Grace readily accepted hers, grateful for the warmth. She enjoyed hearing about the town's history. With the old-fashioned decorations, she could almost pretend she had been transported back in time.

"Ooh," Granny said excitedly. "Over there on the left is where the first bank of Winterwood stood. The bank that my granddaddy started."

Grace looked over to see the old building she was pointing at. It now housed a number of offices for local lawyers and accountants. Grace had known the history behind that particular building for most of her life, but it was still exciting to hear it again. They turned left to head up the side street.

"To the left was the Odd Fellows Lodge. I don't know when it started or how long it lasted, but if you look closely, you can still see the circles with the F, L, and T in them.

At one point, the Masons rented the building, but I believe that was after the Odd Fellows had moved out."

Grace and Hunter peered up at the building, looking for the symbols, excited when they spotted them. Here was history right in front of their eyes.

"Life was sure different back then. You could buy an acre of land for twelve cents. Milk was delivered daily by a covered wagon; the ladies brought their empty pails down to meet it and then returned home with full pails. A local man would cut ice out of the ponds each winter, storing it in an ice house throughout the year. Each day, people would place a card in their window telling him how many pounds of ice they needed, and he would cut it on site. My favorite story is where my mother and grandmother started a Shakespeare's club with local women. They wanted to further women's education and interest in the arts. It was so progressive," Granny said with a wistful smile. "To my knowledge, the club still exists to this day."

Grace smiled; sure, she'd heard something about it at the local library. She had no idea her family members had been a part of it. "Were you ever in the club, Granny?"

"Unfortunately, no. I wanted to, but there was never enough time," Granny said sadly. "I believe this concludes my tour, kiddos. If you're ever interested, the library has a huge section on the town's history, with lots of pictures you can look at. Many buildings have either been torn down or undergone extensive remodeling, so it's interesting to see what things used to look like."

The next time she had some free time, Grace was going to the library. If she was lucky, she might even find some old pictures of some of her ancestors. A lot of them had been lost through the years. Preservation was rarely a thought until it was too late.

They arrived home, Junior helping Granny from the carriage and into the house. Grace and Hunter stayed seated for a few minutes.

"Thank you, Hunter. This meant a lot to me."

"I'm glad it made you happy. I was concerned when you stayed behind earlier. It didn't seem fair that you, of all people, should miss out on this."

"Hmm, since you had no idea that would happen, I believe that means this was not your original 'special surprise.' Now you have to tell me what it was supposed to be!"

Hunter smiled mysteriously, refusing to look at her. "That is a secret for another day."

"Oh, come on," she replied, smacking his arm with the back of her hand. "It's not fair to keep me in suspense."

"Guess you'll just have to beat me at another competition!"

"The bathrooms always need cleaning."

"So they do. Come on, let's get you inside before you freeze to death."

Hunter helped her from the carriage, keeping her hand in his as they walked to the door. Junior left right as they were about to step inside.

"Thanks, Junior," Grace said, giving the old man a huge hug.

"No problem, Grace. Call me if you need anything else," he said with a tip of his cowboy hat.

Hunter and Grace walked inside. "Sounds like we're just in time for dinner," she said.

"It was nice having some quiet time together. We should do it again sometime," Hunter responded nonchalantly.

Grace nodded, unsure of what to say. She would love to spend more time with him, but he was still leaving in a couple of weeks. The last thing she needed was a broken heart. Although, would it really hurt if they hung out once in a while? As friends? The answer was yes, but if she was really going to change her life, why not start now?

-Days till Christmas-

Five

Grace was in the kitchen setting breakfast out when Molly rushed in.

"Oh good, you're still here," she said to Grace.

"I don't need to leave for another ten minutes. Is there something I can help you with?" Grace replied as she measured out the coffee grounds.

"I heard they're planning to discuss the numbers from the festival this past weekend. Is that true?"

"That's what I was told. Why? Do you want to come along?"

Molly nodded her head. "I would like to know if our hard work paid off."

Grace glanced over at Molly as she put the pastries on the platters. "I feel it's safe to say that our Old-Fashioned Christmas Experience has been a success. But I can understand wanting to know how everyone else did, too. Can you be ready in five minutes?"

"I'm ready now. I just need to get my coat."

"Give me a few minutes to finish preparing the food, and we can go."

Grace scooped the scrambled eggs from the container and into the warming tray. She added sausage and bacon and then set several packages of bread and english muffins by the toaster. The fruit bowl was placed in the center of the table, platters of fresh muffins and danishes on either side. Once that was done, she fixed a tray for Granny, which she left on the side of her bed, and then made a tray for Hunter of blueberry waffles and sausage. She dropped the tray off outside his door, knocked softly, and then sprinted down the stairs to grab her coat.

Five minutes later, Grace and Molly were seated at the counter in front of Bea and Addie, who were standing on the other side. There were fewer people there that day. School break had officially begun the Friday before, so a lot of parents were likely still at home with their kids. With most of the activities already over, the excitement faded, and the countdown to Christmas began in earnest. Grace didn't blame them. They had been there when it mattered, and she would forever be grateful to all the people who had so selflessly shown up and given their time and energy to support their town.

Mayor Allen appeared glass and spoon in hand. "Good morning, everyone. It's good to see you all again. I imagine you all have things to do, so I will keep this short. Katie and I spent Monday reviewing the festival numbers this last weekend. I must say, when I saw them, I was shocked, and I think you will be too. Can I get a drum roll, please?" he asked a couple of guys sitting at the table in front of him.

The guys drummed their fingers on the table enthusiastically; it lasted for a few seconds longer than necessary, likely for dramatic effect. Finally, they stopped.

"We estimate that around three thousand people came to the festival on Saturday, with another fifteen hundred or so on Sunday!" the Mayor exclaimed.

The crowd cheered, several people whistling loudly. Grace was shocked to hear the numbers, although when she thought about it, it had been pretty crowded on Saturday, what with the parade and especially the band. They had managed to get a local, fairly well-known group to perform, so it wasn't hard to imagine people showing up just to hear them.

Sunday was a bit more of a surprise, but she hadn't gone, so she had no idea what kind of turnout there had been. The real question is how much money the town had been able to bring in.

Mayor Allen clinked his glass to get everyone's attention. "The city brought in around a thousand dollars in vendor fees, but the real revenue boost will come from the business taxes we'll collect for the fourth quarter in January. We, of course, won't have those numbers until then, but I have no doubt this festival has been a win-win for everyone involved."

They cheered again, Mayor Allen smiling from his position at the front of the room. When everyone was silent again, he turned toward Grace and Molly. "I would like to give a round of applause for Grace and Molly. The driving force behind this crazy adventure. Ladies, if you have any more crazy ideas, please don't hesitate to share them!"

As everyone clapped, Grace blushed, embarrassed by the attention. She was usually the kind of person who blended into the background and was happy with that. These last couple of weeks have pushed her out of her comfort zone. Something she may have to get used to if she was going to get serious about putting herself out there more.

"There are a few more activities to go before the week ends. There will be ice skating at Miller Pond for the next couple of afternoons, breakfast with Santa tomorrow morning, and a Christmas-themed fireworks show Friday night. Those of you who have volunteered to help, please check in with your committee leaders. To all of you, a big thank you and a Merry Christmas!"

Grace watched the mayor book it out of there. He never talked to people after meetings, and she started to see why. People loved to talk. Not only was he the mayor, he was also the pastor at one of the local churches and a real estate agent. A lot of the people in this room were parishioners of his. She could easily see them talking his ear off and him never getting out there if he didn't exit as quickly as possible. She could learn a lot from that man.

Turning to Molly, she held out her hand for a high-five. "Looks like our hard work did pay off," she said with a big smile.

To Grace's surprise, Molly looked more relieved than excited. She was about to ask why when Bea interrupted.

"Are you still planning to help out with breakfast tomorrow morning?" Bea asked Grace.

Grace nodded. "Of course. Do I still need to be there around six?"

"Six would be great. I'll still send some pastries in case some adults don't feel like having breakfast with Santa."

"Thanks, Bea. I'll try to get a head count over to you this afternoon so you know how many to plan for."

"Sounds good. You all have fun ice skating this afternoon," Bea said as she waved goodbye.

Grace turned back to Molly. "You ready to go home?"

Molly nodded, so they grabbed their purses and headed to the car.

"I never asked you how your dinner at Bella's was the other night?" asked Grace as she put the car in gear.

"It went really well. It was very romantic, just as you said."

"Were you able to talk to Grant about your concerns?"

"He said that he's been working remotely on closing out the remaining contracts he handled at work, as well as putting together a surprise for me."

"That sounds exciting. Any idea what the surprise might be?"

"No, and I'm kind of concerned. I appreciate what he's trying to do, but it would be nice to be involved for a change. We're supposed to be partners," Molly sighed. "If he had just told me he planned to quit, we wouldn't be here right now. I just hope this isn't another one of those situations."

Grace wasn't sure what to say. For someone with zero relationship experience, she sure was giving out a lot of advice these days. "I, for one, am thrilled you're here. I can see why you're concerned, but would it be so bad to give him a chance? Maybe he feels like he owes you a surprise or two."

"I can give him a chance. I just hope it ends up being worth it in the end."

Thankfully, they arrived at the house, and Molly got out of the car before Grace could respond to her last statement. She was glad she was single if this was what married life was like. From what she had observed the last few days, ninety percent of problems could be resolved with a conversation. Why that was so hard was a mystery to her, but again, that could be her lack of experience showing.

***

After a quick lunch of hamburgers and fries, they headed to the pond. A company that rented ice skates had been contracted to set up shop near the pond, and, to everyone's delight, they had arrived in a food truck where they not only rented out ice skates but sold coffee, hot cocoa, soft drinks, and cider. They also offered hot dogs, nachos, and chili cheese fries for those looking for a snack. Grace was sure they would make a lot of money over the next couple of days.

Ice skates had been included in the packages the guests booked, so all they had to do was give their sizes, and they were good to go. Grace flitted from person to person, helping out where she could. When they were all finally out on the ice, she sat on a nearby bench to watch. As Hunter completed his first lap around the pond, he stopped in front of her.

"Aren't you going to skate with us?" he asked.

She shook her head. "I think I'm going to sit this one out."

"Why? Don't you like to skate?"

"I don't know. I've never done it before. With my luck, I'll break an ankle or something."

"It's not that hard. Why don't you put some skates on, and I'll teach you?"

Grace looked at all the people gliding gracefully across the ice; even Emma and Theo seemed to be naturals. Then, an image of her falling flat on her face flashed before her eyes, causing her cheeks to flush with embarrassment. "I think I'm better off on dry land. You have fun, though."

Hunter rolled his eyes. "Where's that adventurous spirit?"

"She must have been left back at the house. I'll go get her," Grace said, getting up to leave. Before she could take two steps, Hunter grabbed her arm and pulled her over to the food truck.

"Come on, scardey-cat. It's time for you to try something new."

"What happens if I fall and break something? Who's going to take care of Granny? And who's going to take care of running the inn? I can't afford to take that chance," she protested.

"If you start to fall, I'll catch you. And if, for some crazy reason, you actually do break something, I will personally take over for you until you're healed. Deal?"

Grace shook her head. "I really hope we don't both end up regretting this."

Grace got a pair of ice skates, and Hunter helped her lace them up. When she stood up, she immediately lost her balance and fell into Hunter's arms. If she was honest, this was probably the best part of the whole outing. With a death grip on his arm, she gingerly stepped onto the ice, her feet automatically sliding out from under her. Closing her eyes as she prepared for a hard fall, she opened them in surprise when she found herself pulled up against him instead.

"I told you I wouldn't let you fall," he said against her ear.

Yep, this was definitely going down in the history books as her all-time favorite memory.

"I need you to trust me, okay? If you start to fall, I will catch you. Now that you know that, I want you to relax."

Grace took a deep breath and tried to do as she was told. Her embarrassment at being worse than a five-year-old at something caused a bit of stress and anxiety. When she felt confident enough to stand without falling, she let go of Hunter and relaxed.

"Good. Now, we're going to take this nice and slow. All you have to do is slide one foot in front of the other. Just like this," he said as he showed her how to glide.

Grace waited until he came back and gave her his hand before she attempted to do as he said. She stumbled her first couple of tries before finally getting it. The Olympics were still out of reach, but by the time they were ready to stop for the day, she could at least move in a circle around the pond without falling. It was a win she would gladly take.

After everyone had turned in their skates, they returned to the house for dinner. Grace was not sorry that they were done skating, but she was sorry she no longer had an excuse to hold Hunter's hand. Having that kind of contact with another human being had been nice. One more reminder of how solitary her life had become.

She was starting to understand why Granny treasured her childhood memories so much. It wasn't the fact that it was Christmas or even the activities she talked so much about. It was because she had spent time with her family. For the first time in her life, Grace felt like she was getting to have that same experience, which would make it that much harder when she had to say goodbye. Because, unlike a real family, she wouldn't see these people again. She made a vow then and there to treasure every moment from then on out.

-Days till Christmas-

Four

Five thirty arrived with a bang, literally, when Grace fell out of bed trying to turn off the alarm clock. She was tired, grumpy, and her body ached all over. Who knew ice skating was such strenuous exercise? She sure didn't. She would have tried harder to get out of doing it if she had. Now she had to stand on her aching feet, flipping pancakes, when all she wanted to do was crawl back into bed.

With a heavy sigh, she pulled herself off the floor and dressed. A soft knock sounded on her door moments later, startling her from her dreary thoughts. She quickly threw on her jeans and opened the door to find Hunter on the other side.

"Are you okay? I heard a loud noise and thought I better check on you."

"I'm fine," she replied, her cheeks heating with embarrassment. "I hope I didn't wake you up."

He grinned sheepishly at her. "I'm usually up at this time. Still haven't gotten used to the time change."

"I imagine that will take some time. Well, I'm sorry I bothered you all the same. I'll be out of here in a couple of minutes, so no more loud noises from me!"

Grace groaned inwardly at her awkwardness. It was incredibly sweet of Hunter to check on her, and here she was, acting like a dork. No wonder she'd spent her life single. And why did he get to look so good? She fell out of bed looking like something the cat dragged in, and he got out of bed looking like he was ready for a Calvin Klein commercial. Life really wasn't fair.

"Do you need any help with the breakfast with Santa thing?" Hunter asked.

"We could always use help," she said with a laugh. "These things are always crowded, and we never get enough volunteers. But you're supposed to be a guest, so..."

"So, give me a couple of minutes to get ready, and I'll go with you," he said, rolling his eyes.

Grace nodded and closed the door to finish getting ready herself. A quick glance in the mirror almost gave her a heart attack. She had washed her hair the night before and let it air dry overnight. Her bangs were now a curly mess, sticking out in every direction. Dark circles were under her eyes, and her lips were chapped from being out in the cold so much the last couple of days. It would take a miracle to erase this image of her from Hunter's memory, and she was sure she had already asked for more than her share of miracles.

She didn't have it to spare but took extra time to tame her wild hair and apply makeup to her haunted-looking face. When she felt she looked as good as she could get, she grabbed her purse and headed down the hall, quietly knocking on Hunter's door. He must have been waiting for her because he answered immediately and was ready to go.

They were silent as they walked through the house, careful not to wake the others. Grace had been concerned that if her fall didn't wake them up, their talking in the hallway would, but when she walked by the doors, there was only silence. They were probably as tired as her from ice skating the day before.

Once in the truck, Hunter was intent on driving it as much as possible; they felt they could speak freely again.

"Thanks for coming," said Grace, still too embarrassed to look at him.

"I'm happy to help. This vacation has been nice, but I'm used to being busy. I have found that being idle too long is not good for my mental health."

"Oh no, have I not been providing enough activities? I wasn't sure how much was too much, you know? I didn't want everyone to feel like they would need a vacation from their vacation because I ran them ragged, but I also didn't want everyone to be bored, either. I—"

"Grace, it's okay," said Hunter, interrupting her. He reached over and put his hand on top of hers, giving it a squeeze. "I'm sure everyone is having a wonderful time. I'm just saying that as someone used to working sixty-plus hours a week, all this downtime has been difficult to get used to."

"I guess you'll be glad to return to work, won't you?" Grace asked softly; her heart clenched at the thought of him going back to New York. She looked out the passenger window so he couldn't see the sad look on her face.

"I do like to work," he said slowly. "But I'm thinking about doing something different. This vacation has shown me my life has been lacking balance. Working too much is just as bad for me as working too little."

"What are you thinking about doing instead?"

He squeezed her hand again. "I have a couple of ideas. I'll let you know as soon as I've decided."

Grace nodded. "If you ever need someone to talk to, I'm available. Sometimes, it's easier to talk things out with someone unbiased."

She knew the words were a lie as soon as they were out of her mouth. She was anything but unbiased. If she had it her way, he would stay in Winterwood permanently, but that was unlikely. There were few job opportunities in a town this size. Zero for a man like him. The nearest city was a forty-five-minute commute. Not the worst commute in the world, but not something people usually signed up for voluntarily.

"Thanks, Grace. I'll keep that in mind," he said, interrupting her thoughts.

They pulled up to the community center, and the first thing they noticed was there were only two other cars there. Hopefully, the others were simply running late, but Grace had a feeling that wasn't the case; getting up at five-thirty to flip pancakes is low on people's list of things to do.

Inside, they found Bea and Jenny rushing around. "Thank goodness you're here," said Bea as soon as she saw them. "And thank goodness you brought Hunter. Addie and Junior called in sick, and the remaining volunteers refused to confirm they were coming. So, we have no Santa and no one to help cook or serve the food." Bea's voice conveyed the panic she was feeling.

"Just a wild guess, but I take it you'd like me to be Santa?" asked Hunter, a huge grin on his face.

"Would you?" Bea pleaded. "Oh, please say yes!"

"Of course. How about I help you set up, and then I'll change into the costume? Oh, and help is on the way," he said as he waved his phone.

"Thank you so much," Bea hugged him and then ran back to the kitchen, Hunter and Grace following.

To say the kitchen was in complete chaos would be an understatement. Flour appeared to cover every surface, including Jenny's hair and blouse. Mixing bowls of all shapes and sizes covered the counters while packages of sausage defrosted in the sink. Hunter and Grace looked at each other, their eyes wide with a mix of horror and astonishment.

A few minutes later, the cavalry arrived in the form of Grant and Molly; the two took one look at the situation and immediately took charge. They grabbed an apron, tying it expertly around their waists, and began barking orders like drill sergeants. Jenny and Bea were instructed to finish making the batter, Hunter and Grace were on cleaning duty, Grant started the grill and began cooking sausage patties, and Molly organized the serving tables. Fifteen minutes later, the kitchen was running like a well-oiled machine.

"How did you do this?" asked Bea as she motioned toward the kitchen, amazement in her voice.

"Fundraisers are common in my line of work," Molly laughed. "So, this is not my first rodeo, as they like to say."

"Well, you certainly have my respect," Bea replied as she got back to work.

"Hunter, it's time to get in your costume," Molly called out.

He put down the sponge he was using. "Duty calls," he told Grace with a wink.

She laughed as she took over his sponge duty. Grant was doing a great job manning the grills, while Grace had been relegated to cleaning up after the giant mess Jenny couldn't stop making. "Hey, Grant, were you a fry cook in a former life?" she asked with a wry smile.

He looked over at her and grinned. "Molly's put me to work once or twice over the years."

"I've heard the local Sonic is hiring if you're still looking for a new job," Grace teased.

"I'll keep that in mind," he said, laughing as he flipped another set of pancakes.

When the doors opened at seven, they had a massive stack of pancakes ready to serve, along with a large helping of sausage patties. Grace switched to serving duty and began filling plates while Molly managed the door. They had sold tickets in advance but still allowed people to purchase them at the door. Those same tickets would be collected and then entered into a raffle for a Christmas dinner donated by the local grocery store.

At last count, over five hundred tickets had been sold. At three dollars apiece, they had raised enough money to cover the costs of the ingredients for breakfast as well as to purchase food to take to the elderly they would be singing carols to Saturday night. Of all the events they had put together, this was the one she was most proud of.

Minutes later, Hunter appeared from the back, a full Santa costume in place. With his white beard, padded mid-section, and red suit, he looked enough like Santa that even Emma and Theo should be convinced. When the kids saw him, a massive chorus of 'Santa' erupted as they raced toward him excitedly. Grace couldn't help but smile as she watched him take it in stride, bending down to hug each and every one of them.

Once he could sit down, Grace put a plate full of food in front of him. He was surrounded by kids on all sides, so she stayed quiet and listened to him engage with the excited kids. Someday, he was going to make a fantastic father. The thought caused a sudden wave of sadness, so she excused herself and went back to serving the people in line for food.

Around eight, the group from the inn arrived; Emma and Theo were drawn to Santa like a moth to a flame. Hunter graciously let them sit on his lap and listened attentively as they told him about their trip. He even promised not to forget they wouldn't be home on Christmas, and he needed to come to the inn instead. It was too cute, and Grace made sure to take as many pictures as she could.

Breakfast ended at nine, and they all breathed a sigh of relief when the last diner exited the community center. Despite the earlier chaos and the continuous stream of people, they had survived, and as far as they could tell, all the diners had a wonderful time.

After another half-hour of cleaning, they were officially done. Molly counted the tickets and discovered an additional one hundred people had shown up, increasing their budget by another three hundred dollars. A lot of people would be helped by that money, and Grace was excited to put it to work.

Back in the truck, Grace and Hunter discussed the morning's activities. "What was your favorite part of playing Santa?" Grace asked curiously.

"Seeing the excitement in their eyes. I miss feeling that excited about something. It feels like the older I get, the more jaded I become. It's kind of depressing."

Grace nodded. "I know how you feel. I don't think I've ever experienced that level of excitement. It's embarrassing to admit, but I'm jealous of a bunch of kids!"

Hunter glanced at her from the driver's seat, a serious expression on his face. "Are you serious? You've never been excited about anything before?"

Grace shrugged. "I've been excited about things these last couple of weeks, but that excitement was usually accompanied by a negative feeling. I don't think I've been doing this whole life thing right," she laughed.

"It doesn't sound like it." Hunter parked the truck in front of the house and turned to face her. "What does excite you, Grace?"

She thought about it for a minute, searching her mind for anything to say. When nothing came to her, she gave up. "I can't seem to come up with anything. My life has been very plain and boring. I've been in survival mode for so long; it's all I know."

If she was trying to sell herself as girlfriend material, she was doing a lousy job. Here she was, talking to a successful businessman who lived in one of the most exciting cities in the country, openly admitting to being plain and boring. She had no ambition beyond getting her granny well, no future prospects, and the most excitement she'd ever had was running a Christmas-time inn for strangers. She might as well start collecting cats because she had 'old cat lady' written all over her.

He surprised her by reaching over and playing with a lock of her hair. "I think the problem is you haven't unlocked all your secret desires yet."

She gulped, unsure of how to handle the sudden intimacy. "How am I supposed to do that?"

"Well," he started, seemingly mesmerized by the hair between his fingers. "You need to start by finding the secret key."

Grace opened her mouth to respond when a knock sounded on the window, startling them both. Hunter dropped her hair and turned to see who was interrupting their conversation. When he saw it was Grant, he held up a finger and then turned to Grace apologetically. "Grant and I need to go take care of a few things. Can we resume this conversation later? Perhaps at the pond this afternoon?"

"Um, sure. You really want to go ice skating again?" she asked, trying not to groan. Her muscles were still sore, and the morning's activities had only added to their achiness.

"I love ice skating," he said with a boyish grin. "We have tons of skating rinks in New York, but I never have time to go. Come on, you know you had fun yesterday!"

"I suppose. Let me know when you're back, and I'll go with you."

"It's a date!"

Oh great, there's that word again. She exited the truck and headed inside, more confused than ever. Was there really something happening between her and Hunter, or was she imagining it because she wanted it so badly? And what was that about a secret key? Was he serious, or was he just trying to be nice? Hopefully, she will get some answers this afternoon, and hopefully, she wouldn't embarrass herself anymore.

-Days till Christmas-

Three

Grace awoke in a foul mood. She had spent the entire morning the day before talking herself up to go ice skating with Hunter, only for him to not show up until after dinner. He apologized profusely, and of course, she had graciously told him it was no big deal, but to her, it was very much a big deal. There were only so many days until he went back home, and they were flying by so fast. Christmas was only three days away, after all.

Molly hadn't been thrilled either, as she had hoped to spend time with Grant. Grace just couldn't imagine what they were doing that was taking up so much time. Neither of them lived or worked around here, so what gives? Hopefully, one day, she'd find out.

She went downstairs to prepare breakfast and then hurried back upstairs to check her messages. After several days of messaging random strangers, she'd finally found Carl's brother. At least, she was pretty sure she did. She was waiting, rather impatiently, for confirmation. If he didn't hurry up and respond, there wouldn't be enough time to travel here for Christmas, and she really wanted him to come for Christmas.

After logging on to her computer, she clicked open her email and sorted through the usual promotional offers and spam, finally spotting the response from Edward. She opened it and read through it cautiously, afraid he might turn her down. Instead, what she read brought tears to her eyes:

Dear Ms. Parker,

I apologize for my delayed response, but you gave me quite a lot to think about. As soon as I read your letter, I called my sister Katherine, and we discussed your proposition at length. This rift in our family has indeed gone on too long. In fact, it should never have happened in the first place.

We knew this then, but at the time, we lacked the courage to speak out against our parents. As time passed, I am sorry to admit our guilt and shame prevented us from reaching out to make amends. We would very much like the opportunity to atone for our sins.

Unfortunately, I cannot travel; age and health problems have me confined to my home. My sister, however, is fit as a fiddle and, with your permission, would love to come on our behalf. It is our sincerest hope we can build a bridge with our brother and convince him to come down for a visit so that proper amends can be made. I am enclosing Katherine's information, and if you agree to her presence, I am hopeful you will reach out.

Thank you for showing our brother the love and compassion we have failed to give ourselves.

Merry Christmas!

Edward Richmond

Grace wiped her eyes and checked the time. Seven o'clock in the morning was likely too early to call a stranger. She would have to be patient and wait another hour, which gave her plenty of time to go next door and ask Gladys if she had room for one more.

Grant opened the door and led her back to the dining room, where they ate breakfast.

"Everything okay?" asked Gladys.

"Everything's fine. Sorry to intrude. I just received some information and came to ask for your help."

"You know you're welcome here anytime, dear girl. Here, help yourself to some breakfast," she said as she handed Grace a plate of eggs. "What can I help you with?"

Grace smiled as she accepted the plate, memories from past meals with Gladys flashing before her eyes. "Thank you. I must admit, in all the excitement, I forgot to eat breakfast. I found Carl's siblings," Grace announced.

Grant and Gladys gasped. "Are you serious? I didn't even know you were looking for them," replied Gladys.

"That seems pretty risky," said Grant. "Does Carl know?"

Grace shook her head. "I know it's risky, but I figured the worst that could happen was they refused to talk to me. However, I am happy to announce that the worst case didn't happen. In fact, they agreed that it's time to end the feud and want to make amends!" she exclaimed excitedly.

"That's wonderful," Gladys said, clapping her hands together. "What is it you need from me?"

"Carl's sister, Katherine, is coming here to see him for Christmas. I don't have any rooms available next door, so I was wondering if you have room for one more?" Grace asked hopefully.

"How about this?" Grant interjected. "If Molly is willing, she can move over here with me, and Katherine can have Molly's room. It's about time my wife and I are under the same roof again."

Gladys nodded in agreement. "I think that's a great plan. But if Molly disagrees, we can easily make up another guestroom, so don't worry about that. This sure is turning out to be an exciting Christmas!"

"Indeed, it is," Grace smiled. "It will definitely be one for the memory books!"

"I just hope Carl is as excited about this as you two are. Are you sure he even wants a reconciliation?" asked Grant. He buttered another piece of toast, which he then used as a shovel for his eggs.

"I think he would love one. He told us he's tried several times to reach out in the past but to no avail. Now that his partner's gone, I think he needs his family more than ever."

"I hope you're right. Anyway, it looks like we can add private detective to your resume," he teased. "Your list of skills is growing quite long these days."

"At this rate, I might actually become employable someday!"

"Don't sell yourself short. You've got a lot to offer. Don't ever forget that."

The look on Grant's face was so severe Grace couldn't help but wonder if there was a message she wasn't picking up on. Embarrassed at the compliments, she thanked them and returned home to call Katherine.

***

After making arrangements with Katherine, who will be arriving on Christmas Eve, Grace went to see Granny. Upon entering her room, she found Granny and Molly having a serious discussion. Both of them went silent when they saw her.

"What's going on?" Grace asked cautiously.

She couldn't think of a single good reason for Molly and Granny to have secret meetings. Something must be wrong. Something, for whatever reason, they didn't want her to know. That thought alone brought out a lot of bad feelings. Molly was practically a stranger. Why was she privy to information about Granny that Grace wasn't?

"Come in and sit down, Grace," Molly said, patting the chair beside her. "We need to talk."

Grace was tempted to sit on Granny's bed in a show of defiance but recognized the passive aggressiveness for what it was and sat in the chair instead. Whatever was going on, for better or worse, it seemed she was about to find out.

"Granny has something she needs to tell you," Molly looked pointedly at Granny.

Granny shook her head. "Is this really necessary?"

Grace looked back and forth from Granny to Molly. "Is what necessary? Would someone please tell me what's going on?"

Granny sighed. "I was hoping we could avoid this conversation, but I guess you have a right to know." Granny clutched the quilt in her lap, opening and closing her hands several times as she fought to maintain her composure.

"Whatever it is, it can't be that bad," Grace assured her.

"Always the optimist," Granny said with a smile. "I'm afraid you're wrong this time. I was trying to die," Granny blurted out.

Grace looked at her with wide eyes. "As in suicide?" she asked, shaking her head in confusion. "I don't understand."

"Not necessarily suicide, although maybe that's correct. We're about to lose the house. I can't afford to keep up with the bills and the taxes; it's all too much," Granny shook her sadly. "When I'm gone, you will receive my life insurance policy. It's enough for you to save the house and take care of yourself for many years to come."

"Why didn't you tell me? We could have figured something out. Something that didn't include me losing the only family I have left." Grace choked the last part out, devastated at what she was hearing.

"I spent hours going over every option I could come up with. This was the only one that seemed viable. I'm sorry, Grace. I know this is hard for you to hear."

Grace shook her head as tears streamed down her face. "You knew about this?" she asked Molly. "And you didn't tell me?"

Molly shook her head sadly. "Granny told us the first day we all had lunch together, and I convinced her to give me a chance to come up with a solution. I would have told you regardless, but I wanted to wait until we could solve the problem first."

"I thought you were my friend," Grace said sadly.

"I am your friend," Molly exclaimed. "I never wanted to hurt you, Grace; I only wanted to help. You've had so much on your plate; what would telling you have accomplished? Other than stressing you out to the point of a breakdown?"

"I still had a right to know."

"I agree, which is why we're telling you now. Look, I know you're hurt and have every right to be, but the important part is that I've come up with a plan that will solve all your problems."

It took a minute for Grace to digest everything she had just heard. Her heart was broken. She knew in some strange way Granny was only doing what she thought was best, but the fact she honestly believed the best thing for Grace was to be left alone in this world was gut-wrenching.

"Go ahead and tell me this plan of yours," she finally said, refusing to look at either of them.

"I've done the numbers, and you are going to make enough money from the Old-Fashioned Christmas Experience to pay off the taxes on the house and be able to pay your bills for the next couple of months. My plan is for you to create and offer these 'experiences' during all the major holidays. Mayor Allen has already told us he's on board with any future ideas we have to bring tourists to town. This would be an excellent opportunity to make enough money to support yourselves without turning this into a full-time bed-and-breakfast.

"We couldn't turn this into a full-time bed-and-breakfast even if we wanted to," Grace responded dully. "There's no reason for anyone to want to come here."

"That's why we'll be creating new experience packages. We could also offer wedding packages. There are a lot of possibilities if we put our minds to it."

"Who is this 'we' you keep referring to?"

"You and me. I can help just like I helped you with the Christmas Experience."

Grace turned to look at her, an unreadable expression on her face. "How can I ever trust you again?"

"Grace," Granny said sharply. "You stop that right now. None of this is Molly's fault. It was my decision to do what I did and my decision not to tell you. It isn't fair for you to blame her for my choices."

"She still could have told me," Grace replied petulantly.

"Maybe so, but I made her promise not to. It isn't fair to blame her for that, either. If you want someone to blame, you blame me."

"I need some time to process all this. I'll talk to you both later." Grace got up and hurried out of the room. Tears fell again as she thought about all the time she had spent worried sick about her granny. When she reached the upstairs hallway, she ran into Hunter as he left his room.

"Oh my gosh, Grace, what's wrong?" he asked, concerned.

Grace looked at him momentarily as she replayed the conversation back in her mind. Finally, it dawned on her. "You knew, didn't you?" she accused angrily.

"Whoa," he said, holding up his hands. "Knew what?"

"About Granny. You knew what she was trying to do. Admit it."

Hunter pulled Grace into his room and shut the door. "Yes, I knew, and I'm very sorry. You obviously feel like I should have told you, but Grace, what was I supposed to say?"

"Oh, I don't know. How about the truth?"

"I have wrestled with that for weeks now. A part of me believes you are right, and I should have told you. But a part of me believes we were right to keep it a secret. What good would telling you have done?"

"That's the same thing Molly asked me. Did you two come up with that together?"

"You're being ridiculous," Hunter said, sighing. He ran his hand through his hair. "Look, I know you're hurt; you have every right to be. But none of us wanted to hurt you. Molly begged Granny for time to devise a plan to help, and Granny made us promise not to say anything in the meantime. If I had told you, the only thing that would have changed is you would end up even more stressed out than you already are."

Grace shook her head. "If what you're saying is true, why do I feel so betrayed?"

"Because you were betrayed. But not by me. And not by Molly. We were put in a really awkward situation, Grace. We had only been here a couple of days when we were unexpectedly thrust into the middle of a horrible family crisis. Neither of us was prepared to deal with that, so we did our best and tried to devise a solution instead."

His words hit her hard, and finding she couldn't take it any longer, she broke down sobbing. She turned to flee to her room right as he pulled her into his arms. At first, she tried to fight him but eventually gave in and let him comfort her.

"I truly am sorry," he whispered into her hair.

When she was all cried out, he let her go and handed her a box of tissue.

Embarrassed by her outburst, she sat on the bed and blew her nose. "Thanks," she said, waving the tissue box.

He sat beside her, putting an arm around her shoulders and pulling her close. "It's going to be okay."

Grace nodded, unsure of what to say. Nothing felt like it was okay. Suddenly, she felt exhausted. "I think I need to go lie down for a while."

Hunter reluctantly let her go. "I'll check on you in a little while. You know where to find me if you need to talk before then."

"Okay, thanks," she replied. She got up and left, hoping she wouldn't run into anyone else on the way to her room. A good host was not supposed to disappear in the middle of the day, but she no longer cared. She was in a house full of people, but she had never felt so alone in her entire life. No, she was pretty sure that things would never be okay again.

-Days till Christmas-

Two

There were only two days till Christmas, and instead of enjoying spending it with Granny and her guests, Grace was sneaking around the house, trying to avoid everyone. She had even used the 'death stairs' to escape when she heard someone walking toward the kitchen. It was definitely not one of her finest moments, but she still wasn't ready to face anyone.

She had stayed up half the night, unable to sleep, replaying those horrible conversations over and over again in an attempt to make sense of them, failing to do so each time. The simple truth was they had all betrayed her. They may not have meant to hurt her, but that didn't change the fact they did. It was going to be difficult to ever trust anyone again. Maybe that wasn't fair, but as she had been forced to learn repeatedly, life wasn't fair.

A knock on the door caused her to leap to her feet. She looked around for a place to hide but found none. These old houses didn't come with closets. Sighing, she went to open the door; so much for hiding out in her room all day.

Expecting to see Hunter, she was surprised to find Carl instead. Hunter had come to check on her the night before, but she faked being asleep so she didn't have to speak to him. "Is there something I can do for you?" she asked Carl politely. He was, after all, still a paying guest. If there was a problem, she owed it to him to solve it.

"I was wondering if I could talk to you briefly?"

"Sure. Would you like to come in?" she asked, stepping back from the door so he had room to enter.

"I prefer to talk in my room if you don't mind?"

She shook her head and followed him into the room next door. He offered her a seat in one of the chairs in front of the fireplace. "Here, I made you some tea," he said, handing her a cup.

"You're very kind," she said, accepting the cup. "What is it I can do for you?"

Carl sat down in the chair next to her. "Your absence has not gone unnoticed, and I would like to talk to you about it."

"I'm sorry. I haven't been a very good host. It's just, I haven't been feeling well, and—"

"Grace," he interrupted, holding up his hand for her to stop. "You don't owe me an explanation. I'm not here to complain or judge you. I'm here as a friend."

That got her attention. She seemed to be in short supply of friends these days. "Then why are we here?" she asked curiously.

"I overheard Molly and Hunter talking earlier. I don't know all the details, but I heard enough to know that you're hurting. I'm worried about you, Grace."

Grace tried to smile but ended up wiping tears away instead. "I don't know what to say. My feelings are all so strange and jumbled."

"Why don't you tell me what happened, and we'll see if I can help you sort them out?"

There were so many things she wanted to say, but she didn't know where to start. She took a deep breath and decided to just let it all out. "Three months ago, Granny's health began to rapidly decline. We went to doctor after doctor, but no one could figure out what was wrong with her. The last doctor we saw even told me he didn't expect her to make it through the new year." She could feel tears sting her eyes at the memory of that fateful day.

Carl handed her a tissue box. She had never expected to be the one needing them when she left one in all the rooms. "I knew I had to do something, so I came up with the idea of the Old-Fashioned Christmas Experience. I had hoped that by recreating the memories from Granny's childhood, I could get her up and moving again."

Carl nodded his head. "So, you thought her ailments might be psychological instead of physical?"

Grace thought about it for a minute. "I guess so. I don't think I was consciously thinking of it like that. I just knew I would lose her if she didn't get out of that bed."

"That makes sense, and from what I've seen, your plan has worked. Your granny has been joining us for meals each day, has participated in the activities she can physically participate in, and seems to be enjoying spending time with everyone."

"She was trying to die," Grace blurted out. She looked at the ground to hide her pain. It was too raw to share.

Carl let out a low whistle. "I'm so sorry, Grace. I know that must have been so hard to hear, but you have to understand your granny came from a place of love, even if it was misguided."

"You don't understand. She was doing it because of money. She didn't even give me a chance to figure something out. She was just going to leave me here all alone," she whispered the last part.

"I do understand, sweetheart," he said, leaning forward in his chair to grab her hands.

"Because of your family?" she asked, looking up into his blue eyes. They were just as full of pain as hers.

"No, because of my partner," he sighed. "Cancer isn't cheap, you know. We had insurance but had to meet a high deductible before it even kicked in. Then, when it did, we still had to pay twenty percent. And don't get me started on the prescriptions. We were getting dangerously close to bankruptcy when my partner had the same idea as your granny."

Grace looked at him in horror, and he nodded his head. "The chances of survival were already low to begin with. Going bankrupt just to prolong their life for another six months to a year didn't make sense. At least not in their mind. I still, Lord willing, have a lot of life left to live. My partner didn't want me to spend it suffering financially in addition to dealing with the grief of losing them."

"I'm so sorry. That must have been so hard for both of you."

"I was furious they'd even consider it. I was losing the love of my life. My best friend. Every second was precious. A gift to be treasured. The thought that they would rob me of that gift," he shook his head sadly. "I would have gladly spent every penny I had..." he trailed off, the memories too much to bear.

Grace sat quietly while he gathered his thoughts. Her heart ached for him even more than it already did.

"What I'm trying to say is while it seems selfish on their part, our loved ones feel helpless, and this seemed like a way for them to help. One final act of love they can do for us."

"It still feels so wrong," Grace said softly.

"I agree, and I know how much pain you're in right now. I'm not trying to justify their actions; I'm just trying to get you to see things from their perspective. No malice or betrayal was intended. And while you have a right to your feelings, I don't want to see you wasting precious time being angry at the people who care for you the most."

"I take it you've included Molly and Hunter on that list?"

"I don't know what kind of relationship you have with them, but I know they care a lot about you. They are very worried about you. That much was clear from what I overheard this morning."

"It's all so strange. I haven't known either of them that long, yet it feels like we've been friends for years. That they knew and didn't tell me almost feels like a worse betrayal than Granny's."

"Time moves faster when you live with people," he said with a shrug. "Instead of seeing them once or twice a week, you spend hours together each day. Throw in the fact it's the biggest holiday of the year, as well as the fact you've created this big family atmosphere, and what do you get?"

"Fast friends?" she asked, her eyebrows raised.

Carl laughed. "Something like that, yes. I would like to think we are friends, and I've known you less time than they have."

"Of course, we're friends," Grace smiled. "I keep moping around every time I think about you guys leaving and never seeing any of you again."

"That's not going to happen. The families might move on, but not the rest of us."

"I'm relieved to hear you say that. Now, the holidays won't seem so bittersweet.

"Only if you allow yourself to forgive. Which was the whole point of this conversation. I don't want to see you miss out on the wonderful memories you've been creating because you're spending all your time hiding from the people you should be embracing."

"You're right. I prayed for a miracle, and I got one. Maybe not in the way I expected, but God works in mysterious ways," she said with a smile.

"That He does," Carl laughed.

"Thank you, Carl. Talking to you has really helped."

"I'm glad. You've done so much for everyone else, me included. I'm happy I could return the favor."

Grace stood up and hugged Carl. "Don't forget about the big fireworks show tonight!" she reminded him.

"I'm looking forward to it!"

She left his room feeling like a weight had been lifted from her shoulders. He was right; time was too precious to waste being angry. She was still hurt, which wouldn't disappear overnight, but she was ready to forgive. And the person she needed to start with was Granny.

***

Grace spent the entire afternoon with Granny. Making amends had been easy. She loved Granny too much to stay mad at her. They had then spent some time discussing Molly's plan, only to decide to let it go until the new year and watch a Christmas movie instead. It had been the perfect afternoon, but now it was time to make amends with someone else.

The entire group had walked over to the park for the Christmas-themed fireworks show and huddled together in groups, waiting for it to start. Hunter stood with Grant and Molly but separated when he saw her walking their way.

"Hey," he said awkwardly.

"Hey," she replied.

"Grace, I'm—"

Acting on impulse alone, she stood on her tiptoes and kissed him, cutting off the apology he was about to make. Stunned, she stepped back and looked up into his equally surprised face. "I-I'm sorry. I shouldn't have done that. I don't know what came over me."

He pulled her into his arms. "Does that mean you're not mad at me anymore?"

"I guess not," she laughed. "But I really shouldn't have done that. You'll be leaving soon, and I just made the rest of our time together awkward. I'm sorry."

"Stop apologizing. I'm not sorry, and I don't want you to be either."

"But you are leaving. I don't want to get hurt again, Hunter. Things are hard enough as it is."

"I'm not so sure about that. I told you I was considering making some changes, remember?"

"Yes, I remember, but what does that have to do with me?"

"If I tell you something, you have to promise to keep it a secret. Just for a couple of days. Can you do that?"

"Oh no," she groaned. "More secrets."

"This one's a good one," he said, laughing into her hair.

He continued to hold her close, which made it really hard for her to think clearly. "Okay, fine. I promise."

"Grant and I have decided to start a finance business together."

Grace leaned back to look up at him. "Are you serious?"

He nodded. "Grant already quit his job, and, if you remember, I told you when I first got here, I was ready to quit mine too. We talked and decided we liked the idea of having our own business and being our own boss. No more sixty-hour work weeks unless I want to."

"Wow, I don't know what to say. Does this mean you're moving to Boston to be near Grant and Molly? Because Boston is not that much closer to here."

"If Molly agrees, we'll all be moving here. This means we'll have plenty of time to explore our relationship. That is, if you want to?" Hunter asked. He looked deep into her eyes as if searching her soul for the answer.

Unable to come up with a response, she kissed him again. This time, without fear or concern for the future.

The fireworks started; the noise from the first one reminded her they were in a public place. Embarrassed, she tried to step back and put some distance between them, but he turned her around instead and pulled her back against him. His arms wrapped around her, his chin resting lightly on her head.

They stayed like that as they watched the show; the bright colors lighting up the night sky. To Grace, being in his arms, surrounded by friends and family, was the best Christmas present she had ever had. She was so glad she had listened to Carl. No matter what happened tomorrow, she would always have the memories of the good things that happened today. What more could she ask for?

-Days till Christmas-

One

There was only one more day to go until Christmas. It was crazy to think that only nineteen days had passed since she first proposed the Old-Fashioned Christmas Experience plan. Even crazier to think about all they had accomplished in that short amount of time. Most events like this took months of planning, yet they had pulled it off in only days. She would forever be indebted to all the people who had come together to help make her dream a reality, and that included Molly.

Grace had planned to make up with Molly the night before but had spent her time with Hunter instead. In between kissing, they had spent the night talking about the past and the future. It had been wonderful, exciting, and somewhat scary. She had never been in a real relationship before and still felt way out of her league when it came to him, but he had been nothing but kind, considerate, and compassionate. Hopefully, at some point, she would feel comfortable enough to just be herself around him.

She went downstairs to prepare breakfast and found Molly in the living room. "Hey," she said quietly, careful not to wake Granny.

"Hi," replied Molly. Ruby sat on the couch beside her, her head on Molly's lap. The puppies were curled up in little beds at her feet.

"Can we talk?" asked Grace. There was an awkwardness between them that hadn't been there before. Grace knew it was there because of her and felt terrible about it.

"If you're concerned about me leaving, I plan to be out of here this morning. I'm just waiting for Grant and Gladys to wake up."

Grace shook her head. "That's not it at all. In fact, I don't want you to leave. Grant was the one that offered so Katherine could stay here near Carl."

"What do you want to talk about, then?"

"Look, Molly, I'm really sorry. It wasn't fair that I blamed you for what happened with Granny. I was just so hurt and angry, and it was easier to direct that anger at you. I really hope you can forgive me."

"Of course I forgive you. I'm sorry, too. It was just a terrible thing all the way around. If you're willing, I would be happy to put it behind us and move on."

Grace crossed the room and gave Molly a hug. "I would like nothing more than to put this behind us. Thank you for everything."

Molly hugged her back and then patted the couch next to her. "From what I saw last night, I'm not the only one you've made up with," she said, waggling her eyebrows.

Grace laughed. "Yeah, that was a lot more public than I'd planned. I don't know what came over me."

"I don't know either, but I'm glad it did. It's been obvious there was something between you since I first met you two."

She looked at her in surprise. "Really? I was hoping there was, but I was afraid I was imagining it because I wanted it so bad."

"I would say Hunter's response last night is all the proof you need."

"What about you? Are you okay with staying with Grant? It's been almost two weeks, and you guys are still living apart."

"I'm okay with it. We should have done it sooner. In fact, I'm not sure why we didn't," Molly said with a shrug.

"You've decided to take him back?"

"I think so. I don't know. We haven't talked about the future, let alone made any plans. I love him, but I can't go back to the way things were. I think we can make it work if he's willing to make some changes.

"That's great," Grace replied. She smiled at Molly, glad to hear things were working out with her and Grant. They were both really lovely people, and she wanted the best for both of them. And, if she was lucky, they would turn into lifelong friends.

"Have you given any more thought to the plan I came up with?"

"Granny and I talked about it briefly yesterday, but we agreed not to make any plans until after the new year."

"That sounds like a good idea. Give yourselves time to get through the first experience before you make any plans for a second one."

"Exactly," Grace said, nodding. She was glad Molly understood. She didn't want her to think they were ungrateful for all her hard work.

"When does Katherine arrive?"

"This afternoon. Hunter is going to drive to the airport to pick her up and then bring her back here." Grace took a deep breath and let it out slowly. Out of all the meddling she had done over the last couple of weeks, this one felt the most personal, and extreme. It was one thing to advise a couple to talk, quite another to try to heal a fifty-year-old family feud.

"It's going to be fine, Grace," Molly said, putting a hand on her arm. "Whatever happens, your heart is in the right place."

"Thanks, although that's what Granny said too."

Molly winced. "But even that worked out for the best."

"That's true. So, hopefully, this will too. Anyway, I need to head over to the grocery store. We still need to finish getting the food boxes ready for tonight," Grace said as she got off the couch. She gave Ruby one last pet and then turned to leave.

"Do you need any help?" Molly called out.

She looked back over her shoulder and smiled. "Always!"

Molly got up and met her at the door, linking their arms together as they walked. "Let's do this!"

***

Grace paced back and forth in the living room, looking nervously at her watch every few seconds. Hunter had called a couple of hours ago to say that Katherine's plane had been delayed, and Grace was panicking they wouldn't make it back in time for the caroling that was supposed to start at seven.

Another glance at her watch showed it was already a quarter past six. If they didn't arrive soon, they would either miss the caroling altogether, or it would turn into some weird thing where Grace was like, "Hey Carl, here's your long-lost sister. Okay, everyone, it's time to go caroling." How could she do that to him?

The thunderous sound of multiple feet coming down the stairs caused Grace to stop pacing. She tried to act natural by sitting in a chair by the fire and grabbing a puppy to pet to look less suspicious. When all the guests filed in, she turned toward them and smiled. "What's going on?"

"Is it time to go caroling yet?" asked Chloe, a hopeful expression on her face.

Grace checked her watch again. "I'm sorry. We still have about thirty minutes to go."

"Why can't we go early?" Theo asked in a whiny voice. He threw himself down on the floor dramatically. "I'm so boredddddd."

Grace tried to hide her laugh but was unsuccessful. "I'm sure the puppies would love for you to play fetch with them," she said, covering her smile with her hand.

He perked up at that, picked up a toy, and began eagerly playing with all six puppies, laughing hysterically when they all tried to climb on his lap at once. Soon, Emma was joining in on the fun, and the adults began to visibly relax again.

The sound of the front door opening and closing put Grace back on alert. She stared at the doorway in anticipation, a mixture of fear and excitement churning in her gut. When Hunter appeared, she jumped out of her chair and ran to him, eager to see if Katherine was with him. When she saw the older woman, she gasped. She looked exactly like Carl, only in female form.

Grace took a moment to greet her new guest before calling out. "Carl, could you please meet me in the dining room?"

Katherine, Hunter, and Grace moved further into the room to allow for some privacy. They all turned to watch the door, each holding their breath as they waited to see Carl's reaction. When he entered the room, he looked directly at Grace. "You wanted to see me?"

She was about to respond when the sound of a sob stopped her.

"Oh my gosh," cried Katherine as she ran to Carl, throwing her arms around his neck.

Carl stood still in stunned silence while Katherine cried in his arms. Grace reached for Hunter's hand and held it in a death grip, certain, judging from Carl's reaction, she had made a horrible mistake.

"We should give them some privacy," Hunter whispered.

He pulled her into the living room, shutting the french doors behind him. Twelve sets of eyes turned to look at them in question.

"Carl is meeting with someone in the dining room," Grace explained. "We should still be on track to leave at seven, though."

After a couple of nods, the majority returned to their conversations, and Grace heaved a sigh of relief. She had no idea how she would have explained what was happening in the other room if pressed. Molly, Grant, and Gladys hurried over, eager to find out how it went.

"I think I made a big mistake," Grace whispered. "Katherine cried, but Carl didn't react at all. He just stood there, still as a statue. I've ruined Christmas," Grace cried.

Hunter put his arm around one side of her while Molly hugged her other side. "Let's not jump to conclusions, okay?" Hunter assured her. "He was probably just stunned. The last thing he would have expected is to find his long-lost sister in your dining room."

"Hunter's right," said Grant as he tried to peek through the glass doors behind her. "You probably just gave him quite a shock. I'm sure he'll come around as soon as it wears off."

They stood around, attempting to make small talk while they all watched the clock. It was almost seven, and Grace had no idea what to do. The volunteers from the grocery store were expecting them. The rest of the guests had no idea what was going on, and Grace, try as she might, could not come up with a good excuse to delay the evening's activity. It was going to be very awkward for fourteen people to walk through the dining room while Carl and Katherine were in there.

At seven o'clock, the doors swung open, and Carl popped his head in, grinning from ear to ear. "It's time to go caroling," he sang. "What are you all doing standing around? Our audience awaits!"

Grace's eyes were so wide they almost popped out of her skull. She looked at Hunter and saw he was grinning.

"I told you not to worry," he whispered, squeezing her hand.

The group filed out, everyone donning their winter gear before they headed outside. As the one with the keys, Grace was the last one outside, locking the door behind her.

When she first came up with a list of activities, she handed out a sign-up list to the group at the morning meetings. They were to sign up any elderly or disabled person who lived in town who they thought would benefit from some cheerful caroling. They had put fifteen names on the list. She had then coordinated with the local grocery store to arrange for boxes of groceries to be delivered at the time of the caroling as a Christmas gift. The ticket sales from the breakfast with Santa had been used to fund the purchases. They were to meet the volunteers from the store at the first house, which happened to be one of Grace's neighbors.

They marched up the street, everyone laughing and joking. When they reached their first destination, Grace knocked on the front door, waiting patiently for the elderly man with a cane to answer. As soon as he did, they burst into song, singing Jingle Bells, while the man looked on and smiled. Once they were done, he clapped enthusiastically, thanking them for making his night. Then, the volunteer with the large box of food appeared.

"We have a present for you, Mr. Brooks," said Grace.

He looked surprised but smiled, nevertheless. "That's awfully kind of you, young lady," he said, eyeing the box. "What is it?"

"Why don't you look and see?"

Mr. Brooks looked inside the box and gasped. "This is for me?"

"Yep, it sure is. Merry Christmas, Mr. Brooks," Grace said as she hugged him.

Mr. Brooks looked down at her, tears in his eyes. "Thank you," he said softly.

"You're welcome. Jamie's going to stay and help you get everything put away. Is that okay?"

"Yes, of course. That would be wonderful."

She gave him another hug as Jamie carried the box into the house. After helping him back inside, she turned to the group. "You guys ready for the next one?"

They cheered enthusiastically, continuing on up the street. There were fourteen houses to go, all within about a mile of each other. Luckily, their town was small, so they didn't have far to go. By the time they had circled back home, it was almost nine o'clock. Emma and Theo had long since gotten tired and were carried by their parents. It had been a long night, but one Grace would never forget.

Once everyone was back inside, she checked on Granny and then headed upstairs to her room. Tomorrow was the big day, and she was almost as excited as Emma and Theo. There were only a few things left to do for her special presents, and she couldn't wait to see the looks on everyone's faces when she gave them to them.

"Hey, Grace," Carl called through his open door.

She peeked inside to see him sitting by the fire with Katherine. "Yes, Carl?"

"We just wanted to say thank you," he said, gesturing to the two of them. "I want to say thank you. This is the best Christmas present I have ever received."

Grace smiled at them both. "I'm so happy to hear that. I'll leave you two alone, as I'm sure you have a lot to talk about." She closed his door and opened hers to enter her room, surprised to see Hunter sitting on her bed. "What's up?"

He pulled her into his lap and kissed her long and hard, taking her breath away. When they finally came up for air, he looked her in the eyes. "What you did tonight for all those people," he said, shaking his head. "You're amazing."

"I just did what anyone would do," she replied, embarrassed by his compliment.

"No, you didn't. Not just anyone would have been so kind and caring and thoughtful. All of those people cried, Grace. You touched their lives. Don't dishonor that by downplaying it."

"I wasn't trying to do that," she stammered.

He kissed her again. "I know. You're too modest for your own good. We're going to have to work on that."

He stood up, helping her to her feet. "I just wanted you to know how special you are. Merry Christmas, Grace." He kissed her one last time and left the room, leaving her in shock.

Unsure of what to do, she went to work on the presents. Tomorrow would arrive in the blink of an eye, and she wanted to be ready. It was indeed a Merry Christmas.

-Merry Christmas-

"Merry Christmas!" Grace exclaimed to the crowded living room.

"Merry Christmas," they all replied in unison, causing Grace to smile.

The living room was in chaos, with twelve adults, two teenagers, two young kids, six puppies, and one Ruby, all crowded together, perched on every available surface, including the floor. Yet, it was perfect. She took some pictures, promising to share them with the others as soon as possible.

Stifling a yawn as she had been up since six attempting to get the Christmas turkey in the oven, Grace looked around at all her new friends. "Who wants to go first?"

"I do," Emma and Theo both shouted at once.

"Looks like we have a couple of volunteers," Grace laughed.

The kids opened their presents from Santa, excited that he had remembered they were staying at the inn and not at home. Then they opened the gifts from their parents, all of it taking about five minutes in their enthusiasm. The older boys went next, and they displayed far less enthusiasm until they discovered Santa had brought them a new PlayStation.

She was about to ask for another volunteer when Grant spoke up. "Can I go next?" he asked.

"Sure," Grace replied.

Molly started to hand him his present when he stopped her. "I meant I would like to give you your present," he said, handing her a box.

Molly accepted the present and opened it carefully. When she lifted the lid, she pulled out a framed picture and looked at Grant questioningly. "What's this?"

"It's our new house."

"What? You bought a house? Where? How?" Grace could hear the panic in Molly's voice and instantly became concerned. Even she knew that buying something as big as a house was not a solo decision.

"The house is here in town. I know how much you love it here and hate it in Boston. I want to give you the life you've dreamed of, baby."

Molly's eyes filled with tears as she looked at the house. Grace walked over and held out her hand. "May I see the picture?" she asked.

Molly handed it to her wordlessly, and Grace examined it closely. "This house is just up the street from us," she said excitedly. "We'll practically be neighbors!"

"Really?" asked Molly.

"I thought you might like to be near your new friends. And see," he said, taking the photo from Grace and showing it to Molly again. "It has a nice, big backyard, perfect for children."

Molly covered her mouth with her hand; her tears falling freely. "You did this for me?"

Grant got down on one knee and took Molly's hands in his. "Molly, you are the love of my life. I would do anything for you. Will you stay my wife?"

Molly nodded and threw her arms around Grant's neck. "There's nothing I want more, but what about work? You just bought a house, and we don't even have jobs."

"Hunter and I have decided to start our own business. There are plenty of people around here who could use a financial advisor. Not to mention all the people in the city. And if I'm correct, I believe you have a business opportunity as well," he said, looking at Grace for confirmation.

Grace nodded, thrilled to see Molly was getting her Christmas miracle. They could work out the details later, but Grace had already decided to go into business with Molly. They could even name it the Miracle Inn. They would have to discuss that later.

"I'd like to go next if no one minds?" asked Katherine, pulling an envelope out of her pocket and handing it to Carl.

"What's this?" he asked.

"Open it and find out, silly," she replied.

Carl opened the envelope and pulled out a piece of paper. "A plane ticket?" he asked, looking at Katherine. "You want me to come home?"

"Edward and I discussed it before I came up here. We know this is all very sudden, but we'd like you to start with a visit so we can all spend some time together. Then, if you're interested, maybe you will consider moving back home. We're not getting any younger," she sighed. "We'd like to spend as much time with you as possible."

Carl wiped the tears from his eyes. "I can't believe this. I never thought I'd see you guys again, and here you are, giving me a literal ticket home."

"Is that a yes?" she asked hopefully.

"Definitely," he said, hugging her. "I'm so sorry. I didn't have a chance to get you anything."

"Nonsense. Spending Christmas with my baby brother is all the present I need," she replied, hugging him back.

More presents were passed around until nothing was left under the tree.

"Stay here, I'll be right back," Grace announced. When she returned, she had a stack of presents in her hand, which she then passed out.

Emma and Theo were given toys, while Mark and Michael got gift cards to the Play Store. She then waited patiently for the adults to open theirs.

"Oh my gosh," Chloe said as she opened hers and saw all the photos. "You made memory books for us!"

Grace smiled, glad that at least one person liked them. "One of the things I promised you was memories that last a lifetime. What better way to preserve those memories than with a memory book?" she said, looking at all of them. "I want to thank each of you from the bottom of my heart for choosing to spend your Christmas here with us. You could have gone anywhere, but you came here, and that means more than you'll ever know. Because of you, I got my Christmas miracle," she said as she wiped her tears.

Chloe stood up and walked over to hug Grace. "Thank you. I will treasure this forever. And thank you for my Christmas miracle. I came here hoping to save my marriage, and because of you, it's now stronger than ever."

Grace smiled at Chloe. "I don't think I deserve the credit for that. You and Ryan did all the work. I just gave you a push in the right direction."

Chloe hugged her again and shook her head. "You don't give yourself nearly enough credit."

Janet was next to hug Grace. "I, too, will treasure these memories, and I, too, am grateful to you for our Christmas miracle. Because of you, we were able to make these memories in the first place. Thank you, Grace."

Carl and Katherine took turns hugging her, each thanking her for bringing them back together. By this time, Grace needed a tissue from all the tears. She had hoped they would like her gifts but had never expected this reaction. It was overwhelming, and for someone who was used to blending into the background unseen, it was strangely intoxicating.

Molly and Grant were next, both enveloping her in giant bear hugs. "We're going to be neighbors," Molly whispered excitedly.

"And hopefully, the best of friends," Grace whispered back. "I'm looking forward to babysitting!"

They moved out of the room one by one, each carrying their gifts up to their rooms. The kids were excited to play with their new toys, so Grace was sure she wouldn't see anyone until it was time for the big Christmas dinner.

When she was the only one left, she surveyed the room. Poor Ruby sat quietly by the fire in her bed, looking wild-eyed and exhausted from all the chaos. The puppies played with rolled-up balls of wrapping paper and slobbered all over everything. All that work, and it was over in less than an hour. Sighing, she grabbed a trash bag and got to work cleaning up.

"Grace?" Hunter called from the door.

She turned around to see him. "Hey, what's up?"

"I have something for you," he said, handing her a beautifully wrapped box.

"You didn't have to get me anything," she said, curious what it was.

"Remember that special surprise I promised you?" he waited until she nodded. "This is it."

She opened the box to reveal a bracelet from a well-known jewelry store with the word 'faith' spelled out in the middle of a bunch of charms, each one a symbol of either the inn or an activity they had shared together.

"It's beautiful, but Hunter, I can't accept this. These things cost hundreds of dollars. It's simply too much," she said, trying to hand it back.

He reached out and closed her hand over the bracelet. "It would mean a lot to me if you would accept it. I hand-picked each of the charms. It's special, just like you."

"Hunter, I—" she stopped and shook her head. Wrapping her arms around his neck, she kissed him passionately. "Thank you. I'll treasure it always."

"How about I help you clean up in here, and then we go for a walk? I think getting some fresh air before dinner would be nice."

"That sounds lovely. We seem to work together pretty well," she said, smiling shyly at him.

"A sign of a good relationship," he said, smiling back at her.

"So, it's official? You're really moving down here to start a business with Grant?"

"Yep. I'll need to return to New York for a few weeks, pack up my apartment, and tie up all the loose ends at my old job, but then I'll be back for good. Speaking of which, how do you feel about a long-term renter?"

She looked up at him in surprise. "Like, as in you moving in here?"

"I'm going to need a place to live, and from what I can see, this town doesn't have a lot of options. Renting to me would leave you one less room for guests, but it would give you guaranteed monthly income, so..."

"Yes!" Grace shouted. "I mean, I think that would work," she replied, a little more subdued.

"We should probably talk to Granny first," he said, laughing at her outburst.

"My answer is also yes," Granny said from the doorway to her room. "I think these new plans sound very exciting, and I would like to help in any way I can, including offering rooms to those who need them."

"Thank you, Granny. I'll make sure to pull my weight around here."

"Of that, I have no doubt. Just make sure you take care of my granddaughter. She's the one that matters."

"Yes, ma'am," he said, smiling as he continued putting wrapping paper in the bag.

"Granny," Grace said, staring thoughtfully at a gnome perched on the Christmas tree. "Do you know anything about all these little guys that keep showing up around the house?" she asked, holding up the gnome.

"Of course I do; they're from me."

"What do you mean?"

"Gnomes have always been considered a sign of good luck. I knew how much this meant to you, so I had Gladys go out, buy a bunch of them, and then put them around the house. I wanted you to know I was with you in spirit if I couldn't be with you physically."

"Oh, Granny," she said, throwing her arms around her grandmother. "I don't know what I'd do without you."

"Hopefully, it will be a while before you find out." She hugged her back with as much strength as she could muster.

"I hope so, too. Merry Christmas, Granny."

"Merry Christmas, my little Grace."

Later that day, another miracle occurred when Grace managed to pull off the perfect Christmas dinner. For once, nothing was either undercooked or burned, too salty or too sweet. Of course, she had help from Molly, Katherine, and Gladys, which made all the difference.

They had a lovely time, talking and laughing as they told stories and reminisced about Christmas's past. Grace sat back and tried to imagine what it was like when Granny was a kid, surrounded by all her siblings and cousins, aunts and uncles, parents and grandparents. She'd like to think that it was exactly like this.

Christmas was never about presents, or Santa, or decorations. It was about love, family, and making memories that would be cherished for a lifetime. And that's precisely what they did.

About the Author

Dianna is a wife, mother, reader, writer, and small-town girl at heart. She resides in a rural Missouri town of less than twenty-five hundred people with her husband and three boys in a late 1800s home they've been lovingly restoring when she isn't busy working on her next book.

A romantic at heart, she believes in happily-ever-afters rooted in realism and, most importantly, humor!

She is the author of Forsaking the Dark, a paranormal romance, The Queen's Revenge, a historical romance, and the Holiday Countdown Series, a sweet, small-town romance series.

Afterword

Dear Reader,

Thank you so much for reading Countdown to Christmas! This book came to me on a whim as I was sitting in bed one morning feeling sorry for myself, because, like Greg and Janet, I too have teenage boys that are no longer excited about Christmas. I wanted to capture the essence of Christmas and the memories of our youth, and I am hopeful that I have done just that.

This book is loosely based on the small mid-western town I live in, although any similarities between the town and anyone who lives in it are mere coincidences. Our town is rich in history, having been around since at least 1858, and there is a lot of history to mine. My house, in fact, was built in the 1800s, and has been rumored to have been built by the president of the first bank in our town, just like Granny's. While mine has never been an inn, it was at one point a restaurant that has been rumored to serve

Ernest Tubb and Minnie Pearl! If houses could talk, oh the stories they could tell.

If you enjoyed this book, I would really appreciate it if you would leave a review. I am excited to share that Grace, Granny, Hunter, and the gang have continued their journey with new guests for Valentine's Day, so pick up your copy today!

If you'd like to receive updates on new books, discounts, giveaways, and fun promotions, as well as a free copy of Lessons from a Jilted Bride, signup for my newsletter here: diannahoux.com/sweetromance.

Thank you again for reading.

I wish you all a very Merry Christmas.

Warmly,

Dianna Houx

Made in United States
Cleveland, OH
15 June 2025